"I now pronounce you man and wife."

A funeral-like pause filled the tent. Judge Willis broke the hush with "Brice, you may now kiss the bride."

Kiss?

Prudence felt her heart stop and her eyes widen. Not only did she have to kiss Brice McCormack, she had to make it look good.

Brice's strong, decisive fingers captured her chin and turned her face toward his. She caught a flicker of uncertainty in his eyes just as his mouth claimed hers.

She gasped in surprise at his soft, gentle kiss. The callused pad of Brice's thumb traced the length of her throat. Her heart started to pound and her blood began to flow like warm honey. A fiery ache burned deep inside her.

Gads, her brain was not working at all. Brice was the enemy! Prudence jumped back. She didn't look at Brice. She couldn't, or she just might kiss him again.

Dear Reader,

Welcome to another month of wonderful books from Harlequin American Romance. We've rounded up the best stories by your favorite authors for you to enjoy.

Bestselling author Judy Christenberry brings readers a new generation of her popular Randall family as she returns to her BRIDES FOR BROTHERS series. Sweet Elizabeth is about to marry another man, and rodeo star Toby Randall will let nothing stand in the way of him stopping her wedding. Don't miss *Randall Pride.*

An injured firefighter and the woman he rescued in an earthquake learn about the healing power of love in Charlotte Maclay's latest novel, *Bold and Brave-Hearted.* This is the first book of her exciting new miniseries MEN OF STATION SIX. In *Twins Times Two!* by Lisa Bingham, a single mom agrees to a marriage in name only to a handsome single dad in order to keep together their two sets of twins, who were separated at birth. And enemies are forced to become Mr. and Mrs. in *Court-Appointed Marriage* by Dianne Castell, part of Harlequin American Romance's theme promotion THE WAY WE MET...AND MARRIED.

Enjoy this month's offerings, and make sure to return each and every month to Harlequin American Romance!

Wishing you happy reading,

Melissa Jeglinski
Associate Senior Editor
Harlequin American Romance

COURT-APPOINTED MARRIAGE

Dianne Castell

TORONTO • NEW YORK • LONDON
AMSTERDAM • PARIS • SYDNEY • HAMBURG
STOCKHOLM • ATHENS • TOKYO • MILAN • MADRID
PRAGUE • WARSAW • BUDAPEST • AUCKLAND

To David, David A., Emily, Ann and Gina—
the best family ever. To Leigh Ricker—
best friend and terrific author.
Thanks!

ISBN 0-373-16888-8

COURT-APPOINTED MARRIAGE

This edition published by arrangement with Harlequin Books S.A.

Visit us at www.eHarlequin.com

Printed in U.S.A.

ABOUT THE AUTHOR

Dianne Castell fell in love with the romance genre fifteen years ago when she picked up a Harlequin romance at a garage sale, figuring any book that looked so well-read had to be good. And it was! In fact, it was great! She was hooked on Harlequin romances to the point where she simply had to write one of her own.

Dianne lives with her husband and four kids in Cincinnati, Ohio. When not writing humorous romances, she reads them, watches funny movies, changes kitty litter—which isn't funny at all—sails and collects antique rocking chairs.

"I, Judge H. T. Willis, by the power vested in me by the town of Serenity, Texas, do hereby decree that Prudence Randolph and Brice McCormack, of the feuding Randolph and McCormack families, are hereby legally united as husband and wife. And no matter how much you don't want to be married, whomever I join together better stay that way—or else!"

Chapter One

Prudence Randolph reached across the prosecutor's table and gave her grandmother's hand a reassuring squeeze. She cast a disparaging look at opposing attorney Brice McCormack, and his granddad sitting beside him. Then she faced the front of the courtroom and said, ''Your Honor, my grandmother did not throw a box of nails under the tires of Wes McCormack's red pickup truck and cause him to get a flat. She would never do anything like that. Everyone knows Eulah Randolph's a pillar of the community, volunteers at the nursing home, and is on the library committee. That box of nails slipped out of her hands. She tried to pick the nails up but missed a few. It could happen to anyone.''

Prudence watched Brice roll his eyes. He stood and readjusted his string tie, which always seemed to be in his way. His scuffed cowboy boots made hollow thuds against the polished wood floor as he paced in front of Judge Willis. ''Eulah Randolph deliberately threw those nails under my grandfather's truck, Your Honor. Flattening his tires was a premeditated act."

"That's pure conjecture, Judge." Prudence straightened the jacket of her designer suit as she eyed Brice's attire. Jeans? Again? What kind of getup was that for a courtroom? Especially snug-fitting, hip-hugging jeans. This was not his precious ranch. There were no little doggies running around here to rope and brand.

Prudence cleared her throat. "Mr. McCormack cannot prove his accusations. My grandmother cannot be held responsible for Wes McCormack's flat tires."

"The hell she can't." Brice's outburst was met with a swift whack of Judge Willis's gavel, along with an intimidating look that didn't seem to faze Brice one bit.

It wasn't easy to intimidate a six-foot-four man with broad shoulders and a build to match. Over the past three years, Prudence had tried often enough and had had no more success than the judge. She said, "It's Wes McCormack who's guilty here, Your Honor. He's the one who took *two* tires off my grandmother's Jeep to replace his *one* flat tire. That's larceny."

Brice gave his good-ole-boy shrug. "That's absurd. As you know, Judge, my grandfather is a Boy Scout leader and volunteers with the Head Start Program. He was in a hurry and just mistook Ms. Eulah's Jeep for his own red pickup that needed new tires. Since he was in town he'd decided to—"

"Oh, give me a break, Brice." Prudence glared. "I don't care how busy Wes was—since when can't he tell the difference between a pickup and a Jeep? Your grandfather stole those tires—"

"And your grandmother dumped those nails." Brice towered over Prudence, but she held her ground.

"Prove it!"

"You prove it!"

A loud bang of Judge Willis's gavel echoed through the courtroom. "Tarnation! Enough, you two." His eyes narrowed into thin slits, and his right hand clutched the gavel as if he wanted nothing more than to use it on the two attorneys in front of him. "This damn Randolph-McCormack feud is driving me and the rest of the citizens of Serenity plumb nuts. We've been putting up with it for going on seventy years now, and even by Texas standards that's a mighty long time. Since you two took over defending your kin, I personally have heard every excuse imaginable for one family laying into the other." Judge Willis leaned forward, nearly toppling off his elevated perch. "But today you've both outdone yourselves with the most pitiful, exaggerated explanations I've ever heard in all my days. This nonsense has got to stop!"

Prudence ignored Brice as he stood beside her. "Your Honor," she said in her most attorney-like voice, "this is not the Randolphs' fault. You know as well as I do that if the McCormacks hadn't swindled my granddaddy out of his fair share of the Half-Circle Ranch—"

"Swindle? Ha!" Brice yanked at the silver slide of his string tie, loosening it. "You know damn well that your granddaddy was paid a fair price for his share of—"

Judge Willis whacked the gavel again, this time snapping the wood head clean off the handle. "I said *enough!* We all know what started this feud, and we're not rehashing it in my courtroom. Understand?"

The judge growled as he considered his broken gavel, then he jabbed the headless stick at Grandma Randolph, then Granddad McCormack. "You both should be damn-well ashamed of yourselves for dumping nails and stealing tires. But since I know neither of you are, I'm fining you and sentencing you to clean up Bandstand Park. Wes, you take the north side. Eulah, you take the south. And I *don't* want to hear about any squabbling while you're out there, or I'll have you both slapping paint on bleachers at the high school."

Willis raised his hand to bang his gavel, then realized the futility of his effort. Another of his deep growls echoed through the room. "I've had it with the whole blasted bunch of you. Prudence? Brice? I want you both in my chambers right now, and I mean now. Get your kin out of my courtroom before I get really cranky."

Prudence took her seat and watched Grandma Eulah purse her lips, as Judge Willis left the courtroom, his black robe trailing behind him as if it had difficulty keeping up. ''Well, lordy,'' Grandma said as she smoothed back her neatly styled salt-and-pepper hair. ''Who do you think peed in old Willis's cereal this morning?''

''Shh!''

Prudence gave her grandmother a withering look, which the older woman ignored.

''You'd think this was the first time that old coot, Wes, and myself were in here. Willis should be getting used to this feuding stuff by now. Why, I bet our kin and those no-account McCormacks are in this courtroom at least once a week.''

''More like three times a week,'' Prudence mumbled as she handed Grandma Eulah her purse, then hurried her to the exit. Prudence took care not to crowd Brice, as he led his granddad in the same direction. She spent as little time as possible in the company of the McCormacks and that went double for Brice. Her father had compared her to that boy, that teen, that man, all her natural life. She resented Brice McCormack to no end, and he was her absolute least favorite person in all of Texas.

Besides, another Eulah Randolph-Wes McCormack altercation on the front steps of the courthouse was not a good idea, with Judge Willis in such a cantankerous mood.

Why did he want to meet with her and Brice, anyway? After this latest confrontation, the three of them weren't getting together to exchange chili recipes, that was for sure.

BRICE STRETCHED OUT his legs and settled back into one of the brown leather chairs in Judge Willis's chambers. He had no idea why Judge Willis wanted to see him and Pru. It wasn't like today's court battle was different from any other day's. He didn't have time for this, either. On a ranch, spring meant work, lots of work. Couldn't Wes, Eulah, and the rest confine their spats to wintertime?

He'd gone into law to help understand the oil and ranch businesses that seemed to be getting more and more tangled up in legal mumbo-jumbo these days. Unfortunately, the Randolph-McCormack feud was on an upswing, and defending his kin ate up a lot of Brice's time. Not that he blamed his family, of course. It was those sniveling, whining Randolphs who caused all the problems, and it was his duty to take care of his family.

The chamber door opened, and Prudence entered. She had on another one of those New York power suits. Probably slept in the damn things. Her wardrobe, her pinned-up hair, even her navy-blue Lincoln Continental fit her name perfectly. She reminded him of a store-wrapped package, all done up nice and neat with everything matching and nothing out of place. Sometimes—not very often, mind you, but just sometimes—Brice wondered what was inside the package.

Prudence stopped in front of him. She tipped her chin just a bit to let him know she was all business. Then again, when was Prudence Randolph anything *but* business? "Mistaking a Jeep for a pickup, Brice?

That was really pathetic, especially since Wes was guilty as sin.''

It usually took less than fifteen seconds before she'd start carping at him about something the devil-minded McCormacks had done to the lily-pure Randolphs. He glanced at his watch; today she'd done it in ten seconds flat. Not quite a new record but damn close.

She was really loaded for bear, too. He could tell because her big blue eyes were dark as night, and shooting sparks that reminded him of fireworks on the Fourth of July. When Pru was in a more docile mood, her eyes were the color of those bachelor buttons that grew wild on the side of the road in June. And every once in a while, when he'd catch her off guard, her eyes would be smoky, even a bit dreamy, as if she wanted to be somewhere other than where she was. These days it was hard to imagine Prudence Randolph as a dreamer or as being anywhere but in a fancy business suit in a courtroom.

Brice folded his arms. ''Don't you go throwing stones at my explanation when yours wasn't one iota better.'' He arched his brow in accusation as he mimicked, ''Why, Judge, those nasty tacks just *slipped* out of Eulah's hands.'' He huffed. ''Now that was *really* pathetic, Pru, especially since Eulah was the one who started this whole ruckus.''

He watched her jaw clench. ''For the millionth time, my name is not Pru.''

The first time he'd called her that, they'd been five, and she'd caught him in a game of kiss-and-catch on the kindergarten playground behind the big slide. Even though they were sworn enemies, she'd actually kissed him. And—sworn enemies or not—he'd liked it. For some reason he'd called her Pru ever since.

"My explanation was just fine," she insisted with a toss of her head and a hint of a blush in her cheeks that suggested either she was remembering that kiss behind the slide or, more likely, her defense about the tacks was not fine at all. Between her telltale eyes and her blush, she'd never make it as a big-city, cutthroat attorney—not that she was aiming to be one. Serenity was her home, just as it was his, and they were both aiming to stay here forever, probably doing battle until they were old and gray and using walkers to amble their way around the courtroom.

She said, "Grandma Eulah is just a tad eccentric—"

"A tad?" Brice pushed himself out of the chair.

"And Granddad Wes is the picture of clear-thinking?" Pru's eyes never left his.

"He's...exuberant."

"How about loud and obnoxious, just like the rest of your clan. The whole bunch needs therapy. You spend half your time keeping them out of trouble and the other half solving their problems."

"Better than living in a Randolph dictatorship."

"That's not—"

Pru's words were cut off when Judge Willis stomped into the room. "Damnation!" he bellowed, slamming the door behind him. "You two still at it?'' He peered at Brice, then Prudence, pointing at each of them in turn with his very authoritative finger. ''I want quiet. I don't want either of you to utter one word—not *one*—until I've finished what I've come here to say.''

Brice nodded, and out of the corner of his eye he saw Pru do the same.

Judge Willis said, ''Now sit and listen up.''

Pru took the other brown leather chair, as Brice reclaimed the one he'd vacated. The judge settled himself behind his desk. He still had on his robe, always a bad sign. It meant he was going to use his judicial power for something, and that something was never good for attorneys.

Judge Willis deliberately placed the head of his gavel on one side of his large, oak desk and the handle on the other side. His thick eyebrows drew together into one long, furry line as he studied the two pieces, then said, ''Things in Serenity are going to change. This feud is going to cease and desist. And you two—'' he gave Brice and Prudence a penetrating look ''—are going to make it happen.''

Knowing that was impossible, Brice felt words of protest forming on the tip of his tongue, and watched Pru swallow away protests of her own. Judge Willis was the final voice of authority in Serenity, and everyone knew it. He was respected. He never backed down. He took no sides in the feud, and he always wanted what was best for the town.

The judge pushed his chair back, then paced. His footsteps were soundless on the well-worn Navajo rug now splashed with late-afternoon sunlight. "I've given this a lot of thought, you see. I've got a plan that's going to solve our present problem. You two are going to work together." He nailed them both in the same glare, silencing any rebuttal. "And I do mean *together.* I want you to get one member of each of your families talking—not yelling, screaming or hurling insults—with someone from the other family."

Brice opened his mouth, then snapped it shut. He would argue later.

The judge continued. "Think of the most easy-going, agreeable relatives you have, get them on neutral territory—maybe have them meet up in another town. You two make sure they get together, maybe have a little dinner, and everybody communicate like civilized people! It's the first step in putting a stop to this dang feud."

Pru said, "But Brice and I—"

The judge scowled a warning. "No buts! You're going to get two people talking, and then they can get two more, and so on. And—" his expression hardened, his face turned a little purple, and he pointed that authoritative finger again "—if you two don't cooperate, the next time your grandmas and granddads and aunts and uncles and cousins come into my court over some altercation, they're not just paying fines and doing community service. *They're spending time in jail.*"

Brice heard Pru's gasp at the same time he gulped.

Jail? McCormacks didn't go to jail. Randolphs didn't, either—though they sure as hell should.

"I'm not just blowing smoke here," the judge said. "I mean every bloomin' word I'm saying. The town is splitting right down the middle because of this feud. Wasn't so bad long ago when only a few people were involved. But as more McCormacks and Randolphs married and had kids, and then those kids married..."

The judge shook his head, setting free strands of gray hair that had been carefully combed over an ever-expanding bald spot. "Damn near the whole town's involved now. You know my own daughter's married to a McCormack and my niece to a Randolph. But what you don't know is what it's like at my house when those two girls wind up there at the same time. Sweet mother! And to think they used to be best friends. My ears ring for days after one of their tiffs." The judge looked bleary-eyed and rubbed his temples.

He checked his watch. "I'm sequestering you both in here for an hour, and I want results. You understand me? Three days from now I want to hear that two people from your families met and that all went well. Then they can think of two more people to get together."

The judge strode to the door. When the door shut behind him and the tumbler turned, Brice knew the judge hadn't been kidding. And when a pencil hit him in the arm he knew this wasn't just some bad dream. ''Why'd you throw a pencil at me, Randolph?''

''You put Willis up to this, didn't you.'' Pru's eyes were blazing.

''Me? What gives you that idea?''

She got up and kicked her briefcase across the room. ''Because the McCormacks are tired of hearing what a worthless bunch of conniving thieves they really are and want to hush up the whole sordid ranch deal.'' She shrugged off her jacket and tossed it over her chair.

''Maybe you put Willis up to this because the Randolphs are running out of things to whine about. Whine, whine, whine, that's all they ever do. Owning half the town isn't enough.''

''You should talk. Operating half of one of the most prosperous spreads in these parts wasn't enough for the McCormacks—they had to go and steal the other half, as well.'' She rounded on him, the toes of her high heels touching the tips of his boots. She planted her hands on her hips—her very shapely hips. Criminy, where'd they come from? He never took notice of Pru's hips before. Until right now he hadn't realized she had hips.

Oh, he'd been close to her enough times, just couldn't remember ever being at hip-eye level. Hmm. Usually he and Pru were stomping around, exchanging hostile looks, accusatory glances and incriminating barbs. They didn't spend any time alone. Except for a few minutes here or there, this was a first. For sure, they'd never been locked up together with him looking at her hips. Suddenly, Brice's hands itched to be where Pru's hands were.

"We didn't *steal* the Half-Circle," Brice said, desperately trying to forget about rounded hips, itchy hands and being alone with Prudence Randolph in such a small room. "The ranch was bought and paid for, and it wasn't the richest spread around seventy years ago—you can bet your bottom dollar on that. My family works to make it successful."

"When you can keep them out of trouble long enough."

Brice's glare clashed with Pru's at the same moment the door opened, and Judge Willis stuck his head inside. "You now have fifty-seven minutes to comply with the wishes of this here court—that's me, in case you've forgotten—or you're both going to jail for contempt. Then you'll be able to give your families a firsthand report on the conditions there!" The door banged shut behind him.

"Damn." Brice didn't know if he uttered the word first or if Pru did.

"Now what?" she said as she paced. Brice snatched his briefcase out of her path. It was his favorite, and he didn't intend to have Pru drop-kick it across the judge's desk.

Her perfectly pinned-up hair was loose, trailing around her face in little spirals. She looked sexy as hell. He gave himself a mental shake. Being locked up alone with Prudence Randolph was doing strange things to his brain, as well as having a decided effect on parts of his male anatomy that were nowhere near his brain. He made a mental note to never get locked up with Pru again.

"Now," he said, reining in his wayward thoughts, "we come up with a McCormack and a Randolph who can be in each other's company for more than thirty minutes without all hell breaking loose."

"Impossible," Pru said, as he caught a faint whiff of vanilla perfume.

It was Pru's scent. He'd noticed it enough times, smelling up the courtroom. Sometimes it made his insides clench the way they did when he drank ice water too fast. Sometimes it gave him cravings for vanilla wafers, pound cake, or even a vanilla soda over at Dusty's Malt Shop. Today his stomach flipped, and he had a terrible urge for all three. Hellfire, being cooped up with her was driving him nuts. He had to get out of here fast!

Prudence watched Brice shove himself out of his chair and walk to the other side of the room. It was actually more of a tramp. He undid the top button of his neat, western-cut, navy shirt and ran his long fingers around the inside of his collar, pulling the material away from his neck. She noticed the skin there was as tanned as his face. It wasn't the deep bronze of late summer but a mere kiss of brown from the sun of early spring. Kiss? She licked her suddenly dry lips and stared at Brice's neck. Where had this kiss stuff come from?

He flexed his shoulders as if attempting to ease some tension building there. It might have worked for him, but the simple gesture did nothing to ease the tension building in Prudence. This was crazy. Brice was her arch rival, the person who'd made her life miserable for as long as she could remember. He was the person her father had always held up as an example of what she should be. Since her father was the unofficial head of the Randolphs and she his only child, she had to be as good or better than a McCormack ever even thought about being. And that meant better than Brice-the-perfect, son of the unofficial head of the Half-Circle.

Considering all that, she had never before actually thought of Brice's neck—except maybe in the context of putting a noose around it and pulling tight. She definitely never thought about it in relation to a kiss. She swallowed. It must be their current confined circumstance.

In court she had no problem ignoring his brown eyes, the tiny scar above his left brow, the way his black hair curled slightly over the back of his collar, his rugged build that was nothing like those of the businessmen she came in contact with. But today he reminded her of the cattle he raised—strong, solid, prime, grade-A beef. Suddenly, she had the urge to sink her teeth into his butt. Damn! She had to get out of this room!

"Janet Lowry."

Brice whirled around to face her. "Huh?"

"Janet Lowry. Librarian. My Uncle Walt's middle child. Completely agreeable to everyone. Would just as soon choke as say an unkind word, even to a McCormack."

Brice gritted his teeth and pulled in a deep breath, broadening his chest even more. Prudence bit back a carnivorous whine.

"Blake Edwards," Brice said. "He's my aunt Freda's youngest. Works with Doc at the vet clinic. You can't find a more polite guy."

Pru nodded and went to retrieve her briefcase from the middle of the room. She tried not to think of Brice's broad chest, tanned neck and delectable backside. It wasn't easy. At least the ordeal of being alone with him was finished. Judge Willis had his two names, and maybe—if miracles still happened—the Randolph-McCormack feud would subside, and she'd never think about Brice McCormack's hair, eyes, neck, chest and butt again.

THREE DAYS LATER, Brice watched Judge Willis pace his chamber, mad as a hungry cow grazing on AstroTurf. He glared at Prudence sitting in one leather chair and Brice occupying the other. "This dad-blasted feud's worse than ever, and you two are to blame."

"Us?" Prudence said, her voice sounding a bit breathy, making Brice's blood flow a mite faster. "None of this was our idea," she continued. "We didn't cause that altercation over in Springfield. Blake and Janet did. How could the cowboy here—" she nodded at Brice "—and I know the sheriff would have to be called in to break up a Randolph-McCormack food fight?"

Damn, he didn't need to hear her sexy voice. And

why did she have to call him 'cowboy'? It stirred up old memories better forgotten. The first time she'd called him that was after he'd kissed her the second time. They were six, and he was riding in his first rodeo. They'd run into each other in a deserted area behind the grandstand. For some reason he still didn't understand, he'd pulled one of her braids when she walked by, and when she turned around he'd kissed her. She hadn't moved but her eyes were as big as saucers. And when he ran away, she'd called, "Good luck, cowboy."

Hellfire! He thought being away from her for three days would end this sudden, unexplainable burst of Prudence lust, but today he was lustier than ever—more than he'd ever have thought possible—over Prudence Randolph. He had to stop this and concentrate on her as an opposing attorney, who was always snapping at him over something and acting as if it was her God-given right to do so. He'd have to remember her as the thorn-in-his-side Randolph who made his life hell. In fact, she seemed to enjoy making his life more of a hell than she did the life of any other McCormack. If he remembered all that—and not her eyes, her lips, her hair—he'd get over her in no time.

Judge Willis poked his finger at Pru. "You know you're responsible for the mess in Springfield because you chose Janet." The judge peered at Brice. "And you chose Blake. And neither of you showed up to get their first meeting off to a good start."

Brice said, "Judge, the spring rains had cows and calves caught in mud holes and—"

"And," Pru interrupted, "it's tax time, and I had to get extensions on—"

"Poppycock! You both sabotaged my plan on purpose, thinking I'd change my mind about ending this here feud, didn't you."

Pru held up her hands as if fending off a charging herd. "Not me, Judge."

"Don't look my way," Brice said.

"Well," the judge groused. "We're going to come up with two more candidates, that's all. And this time it's going to damn well work."

Pru squirmed in her chair, sliding the black skirt of her perfect black suit up her very perfect thighs. She had on black stockings, and for a moment Brice forgot about feuds and judges and could only think about what was holding those stockings up. Garters? His mouth went bone dry. Pru would look great in a black garter belt and black stockings, especially if that's all she wore.

He stole another quick look, mostly because he couldn't help himself. Damn, she had long legs, great calves, terrific thighs and...and a tattoo? Brice blinked twice to clear his vision. Yep, it was a tattoo, all right. A rose tattoo peeking out from under the hem of her skirt.

Damn! He and Pru had to quit meeting in this blasted room. There was something about Willis's chamber that got him paying attention to and thinking about stuff he would be better off completely ignoring. But what man could ignore a rose tattoo, black stockings and a garter belt?

"Mr. McCormack!" The judge bellowed, making Brice's head snap back. An exasperated expression covered the judge's face. "If you're finished day-dreaming about...about..." The judge stopped talking, then looked from Brice to Prudence. Willis's eyes suddenly brightened, and his shoulders relaxed.

"I'm listening. I'm listening." Brice yanked his thoughts back to the matter at hand. Too bad his body didn't follow. He set his briefcase on his lap, trying to look professional instead of totally turned on. Ending this feud was killing him.

Brice cleared his throat and said, "Your Honor, maybe you should give this idea of yours a rest. Really consider if there *are* two people who could make your plan work."

Out of the corner of his eye, Brice could see Pru nodding. Judge Willis was quiet, studying Brice as if he'd never seen him before. Then the judge looked at Pru the same way. What was going on? Something was up that gave Brice a queasy feeling.

Finally, Willis said, "You know, maybe you're right."

"I am?" Brice breathed a huge sigh of relief. Nothing was up, everything was fine. He and Pru would be out of here in no time, and he could get back to branding calves. "We'll think of some other way to end this feud. I was thinking—"

"Nonsense," said Willis. "We don't need another plan. It's the two people we get together who have to make this plan work. You just chose the wrong people."

Pru said, "But no McCormack and Randolph can get along."

The judge stroked his chin again, and a tiny smile tugged at the corners of his mouth. "I'm not so sure." The smile grew. "Fact is, this time around *I'm* doing the choosing. You see, if two people are going to get along, they should be used to each other's ways, used to compromising and not fighting at every turn the way Blake and Janet were. Isn't that right?"

Brice shrugged in agreement and watched Pru do the same, as she said, "But that's the point—"

The judge continued as if she hadn't uttered a word. "And these two people should know the value of give and take, how to fight fair, how to choose their words carefully in delicate situations. Correct, Mr. McCormack?"

Brice nodded, but for some reason the judge's smile was evolving into a grin that made Brice's queasiness return.

"I think—" the judge faced Prudence "—the two people who are going to initiate an end to the feud should be well-acquainted. That way there'd be no surprises in store, no period of adjustment. They'd know right off the bat what they're getting into. Agreed?"

Prudence bobbed her head, but there was suspicion in her eyes.

"And most important," the judge said, his voice

rising, ''these two people need to know I want this feud to end, and that I always get my way. They need to know I mean business. They must put the welfare of their families before all else, even their own preferences, and it would seem wise to get two people who are leaders in their own families.'' He looked from Brice to Prudence. ''Get my drift?'' Then he gave them a big toothy grin.

''No!'' Brice said the word at the same time Prudence shouted it, jumping to her feet. Brice felt a heavy thud beating where his heart should have been. ''Pru and I are not the two people needed to get the families together. All we do is argue, incessantly.''

Prudence was hyperventilating. ''I...I agree. No one would believe Brice and I are suddenly getting along, that we're suddenly...friends.''

''Oh, not that, not that,'' the judge said, wagging his head. ''I don't think there's much to be gained by you two posing as friends.''

Brice felt as if the entire state of Texas had just been taken off his shoulders. A faint touch of color returned to Pru's pastey-white cheeks.

''We need something more,'' the judge continued.

''More?'' Brice braced himself. Pru looked paler than ever.

''Much more.'' The judge perched himself on the edge of his desk. ''I'm thinking...marriage. It's the very thing needed around here to bring the Randolphs and McCormacks together, literally.''

''Judge—''

Brice's protest was cut off by a wave of Willis's

hand. The judge said, "Both of you are destined to head up your families. You're the logical choices."

Prudence was opening her mouth but nothing was coming out. She looked like a fish out of water.

The judge folded his arms and straightened his spine. He beamed. "Congratulations, Prudence and Brice, on your upcoming nuptials."

Chapter Two

Prudence felt her jaw drop, her feet go numb and her eyes nearly pop from their sockets. ''But...but...'' She couldn't think of another word to go with *but.* Brice looked as if he'd been kicked in the head by his prize bull. The judge looked as if he'd just won the Nobel prize for Peace and was about to deliver his acceptance speech.

''I'll get the paperwork going now,'' said Judge Willis, ''and you two can get married on Sunday.''

Brice choked. ''You want us to marry in three days?''

The judge nodded. ''Yep. Don't want to give your families time to set up a kidnapping or hatch some other scheme that'll waylay this crackerjack idea of mine.'' The judge stood and looked out the window at the town square striped with daffodils blooming in neat rows and new buds festooning trees older than he was.

Under the circumstances, Prudence couldn't imagine how Serenity could look so...normal. Nothing was normal, blast it. Everything was haywire.

The judge continued. "The wedding's got to be big, the reception that way, too. We'll have it at my place—I'll officiate." He looked at Prudence. "An outside ceremony. The missus will be your nonpartisan attendant. Sunny just loves weddings, and besides, she'd do anything to end this feud since she wants me to retire. I sure as blazes can't do that with Serenity divided two ways to Tuesday." Satisfaction shone in his gray eyes. "This will work just dandy. Never knew a Randolph or McCormack that wouldn't show up at one of their own kin's weddings. It'll bring the families together, get 'em all talking."

"Get 'em all fighting," Brice said. "You can bet on that. It'll be a knock-down-drag-out free-for-all, and your place will be leveled. Do you have disaster insurance? If not, forget this."

"I'm not forgetting it, and nobody would dare cause a ruckus at my house if they know what's good for 'em." The judge shook his head. "Since neither of you is romantically involved with anyone else—and I'd know 'cause my Sunny keeps up with that sort of thing—this is the perfect solution. You two'll just have to do a bang-up job of convincing the families that you're in love and have kept it secret for as long as you could, but that you just can't hold it in anymore, and nothing can ever break you apart." The judge nodded in satisfaction. "That sounded pretty damn good, if I do say so myself."

Prudence wrung her hands, mostly to keep from strangling the judge. "Your Honor," she started in as calm a voice as she could muster, "as you very well know, Brice and I can't spend five seconds together without getting into an argument."

Brice shrugged. "Actually, the record's fifteen seconds, but that still doesn't make much of a case for marriage. Who's going to believe that the two people in this town most hostile toward each other are now in love?"

Judge Willis waved his hand as if shooing away a gnat. "Tell 'em it was a cover-up. You pretended to argue in public to hide what was really going on between you. You knew the families wouldn't condone it. Now you simply have to make your love known to all because it's gotten bigger than both of you, bigger than both families, bigger than the grand state of Texas."

"No one's going to buy that hogwash," Brice yelled.

Judge Willis's eyes narrowed with determination. It was the kind of look he had before he tossed some law-breaking varmint in jail and threw away the key. "Unless you two can come up with an alternative idea to ending this feud, *or* you don't mind holding all future family reunions in the county lockup, you're getting married in three days and your families are going to believe you are madly in love." He banged his fist against the desk. "This case is closed."

PRUDENCE STAGGERED out of the courthouse, dropped her briefcase on the top step, then plopped herself down beside it. She leaned against one of the big white, fluted columns supporting the gabled roof overhead. Maybe she should have checked her horoscope today. Maybe it read, "In three days you're marrying Brice McCormack. Run for your life!"

For as long as she could remember, that guy had made her life hell. He may not have been aware of it, but that hadn't altered things one bit. If Brice was editor of the school newspaper, Dad expected her to be editor of the yearbook. If Brice took advanced math, she had to. Brice went to college and was a business major, so she had to do the same. It even followed to law school.

Randolphs had to keep up with McCormacks, her dad had said, but she always felt as if she fell a bit short. Not that she'd ever admit that to a living soul. In high school she'd prayed Brice would just take one measly course in watercolors, painting or ceramics. She would have settled for a class in clothing and construction. It never happened. Her only consolation was that the high school hadn't allowed girls on the football team, so she'd escaped being a quarterback, running back or some other back. Prayers are answered in mysterious ways.

She turned around, just as Brice came out of the courthouse. The town clock bonged the five o'clock quitting time. "Okay, cowboy, I—"

"Pru, if we start arguing now, we'll never figure a way out of this." He didn't look down at her, but studied the street in front of them, busy with afternoon traffic. The splashing fountain in the town square across the way couldn't be heard over the hum of the cars, but sunlight sparkled off the ripples of water. Prudence heard someone inside the courthouse lock the big wood doors, indicating Serenity's civil servants were through serving for the day and were going home to their suppers, leaving her and Brice alone on the porch to contemplate their fate.

"I was going to say," she said, "that I think we should stay calm and come up with an alternative to Willis's plan."

Brice gave her a sidelong glance, and his left eyebrow—the one with the tiny scar—arched in surprise. "Thought you'd be pitching a fit."

"I never pitch fits. I have...opinions."

"Amen to that. The one thing I do know for sure, Pru, is that come hell or high water, we're not getting married."

Considering the circumstances, the fact that he'd called her Pru didn't bother her. "*That* we agree on. Now we just have to think of a way to end the feud, and we have to do it in less than three days. Got any brilliant ideas?"

A spring breeze ruffled Brice's black wavy hair. He slid his well-worn Resistol on his head. He'd had that hat for ten years now. He'd gotten it for his twenty-first birthday, Prudence remembered. She could still see him strutting down Main Street as if he didn't have a care and owned the whole world.

But that was a long time ago, before Brice went to law school, before his daddy died and he had to return home before graduating to run the Half-Circle, before that ranch and his family became his life, and *way* before he faced a shotgun wedding to Prudence Randolph.

"We could," she offered, "just tell our families what's going on with Willis. We'll tell them that if they don't quit squabbling, the judge will toss the lot of them in jail." She nodded, liking this idea the more she thought about it.

Brice sat down across from her and leaned against the next column. He stretched out one leg, bent the other at the knee. He slid his hat farther back on his head and looked at her. Tiny creases—the kind people who spend their life in the sun get—fanned out from the corners of his mouth and dark eyes. "You know as well as I do, that won't stop the feuding. The families will just keep at it, and when they get to jail they'll fight more."

"So what's your brilliant idea? Huh?"

"First off, we're going to tell our families that we're getting married. If we don't, Judge Willis will, and then there really will be hell to pay. If *we* do the telling, at least we can defuse things a bit."

"Good grief, McCormack! That's it? That's all you can come up with? What kind of a dumb plan is that?"

"Okay, Wonder Woman, you think of something." He gave her a long, lazy look. The kind that suggested he was a blink away from falling asleep. Of course, that wasn't what the man was feeling at all. Over the years, Prudence had come to realize that in times of crisis, the calmer Brice McCormack was on the outside, the more agitated he was on the inside. Of course, the reverse also applied. That meant when he was doing battle-royal with her, Brice McCormack was feeling fit as a fiddle. Blast the man, because when she was in court she was usually tense as a cat at a dog show.

Prudence sat for a few moments, searching for a solution and feeling totally brain-dead. "So I can't think of anything, either. Maybe when we aren't so addled we'll be able to think of some way out of this. We do have three days."

"Yeah, and it took God seven days to create the Earth, and that was a piece of cake compared to what we're trying to do. I suppose the best thing is for you to tell your family, and I'll tell mine. That way we can each live to see tomorrow's sunrise. When we think of a way out, we can tell them we changed our minds."

Prudence exhaled a deep breath. "We can't announce to our families that we're getting married without both of us being there, Brice. If you're not with me when I let out this little piece of news, my family will think either I'm completely off my rocker, or I'm just pulling their leg. Your family will do the same."

"Actually, they'll just have me committed."

Brice stretched out his other leg and heaved a deep contented sigh that meant he was anything but. His worn boots needed a shine, his jeans molded his muscular thighs and area right above his thighs. Oh, dear. Prudence didn't care about the boots. She tried not to pay attention to the jeans and the molding. She didn't have much luck.

Why was she suddenly noticing Brice McCormack—the man—these days? Before, he'd just been Brice pain-in-the-backside, eternal-enemy McCormack. This was all Judge Willis's fault. Until he'd locked her up with Brice, she'd never noticed his molded jeans. At least, she hadn't noticed them the way she was noticing now. This had to stop. She refused to be attracted to a McCormack, especially the very one she disliked the most.

"We're telling my family first," she said. "Randolph House is only two blocks from here, and I don't want a McCormack phoning Dad, telling him about the marriage. That's exactly what's going to happen if we tell your family first."

Brice's brown eyes widened. "And you think *your* family won't call *mine,* making them madder than a nest full of hornets poked with a stick?"

Prudence flicked a dust particle from her suit jacket. "Randolphs have better manners than to ever do something like that."

"I must have forgotten that throwing nails to flatten tires is the epitome of good manners. We'll flip to see which family is told first," he said, disarming her protests as he plucked a fifty-cent coin from the watch pocket of his jeans. "Heads," he called, and flipped the coin in the air, catching it in his right hand. "Ah gee, sorry, Pru." He nodded at the coin showing heads.

"Huh. You're not sounding too sorry to me."

''Looks like we'll be visiting the Half-Circle first.'' He slid the coin back in the little pocket. ''Tough break.''

Prudence snorted. This was a red-letter day in tough breaks. She stood, dusting off the back of her skirt. ''Well, it's late. I'm getting hungry, cook's fixing pot roast, so let's get on with it, then I can get home to dinner. I sure hope she has something chocolate for dessert. Got any words of wisdom so the McCormacks don't shoot me and throw my carcass over their fence post as a warning to other Randolphs?''

Brice stretched as he stood, pulling his dark maroon shirt tight over his six-pack stomach and broad chest. Prudence managed to swallow an unexpected whimper of pure appreciation.

''Well,'' Brice said, setting his hat more firmly on his head. ''Now that you've asked—providing Mamma lets you inside the house at all, go in the living room. That's sure to keep you safe.''

''Why?'' Prudence picked up her briefcase. ''Is it against McCormack hospitality to shoot Randolphs inside?''

''Hell, no.'' Brice picked up his briefcase, and they started down the steps. ''McCormacks would just as soon shoot a Randolph in one place as another. But Mamma just got new carpet in the living room, and she'd be real ticked if someone got Randolph blood all over it. Just don't go in the hall. Carpet there's not worth two cents, and Mamma doesn't give a hoot in hell what happens to it.'' Brice gave her a quick wink, just as she gave him an elbow in the ribs.

AS BRICE APPROACHED Judge Willis's house, he tried to ignore the spacious, white tent set up on the front lawn, and the bakery, flower and rental trucks lined up in the driveway. He pulled at the starched collar of his tux shirt as he drove his pickup around the side of the house. In spite of all the judge's preparations, Brice was sure he'd never get married today; he'd strangle to death in this ridiculous penguin suit before he ever took the vows. Considering the two events, death wasn't looking so bad.

How could this be happening? Brice wondered as he parked, then got out of the truck. How could he and Pru—both intelligent people and wizards at thinking up ways to get people out of messes—not have thought of a way to stop their own unwanted marriage and avoid getting their kin tossed in jail? He was early, the ceremony wasn't till four, but he had to see Pru one more time before the judge pronounced them…his brain refused to compute those three little words.

Brice ran his tongue over his back molar, checking to see if it was still loose from that lucky punch thrown by Pru's uncle Roy after they'd told the Randolphs about the impending marriage. Brice had been ready for the fight of the century, knowing full well he'd probably come out on the short end. Businessmen or not, he suspected he'd have a tough time fending off the whole blamed Randolph family. But when things got ugly, Pru had literally stepped in beside him and stopped the fight before it began—well, except for Roy's one lucky punch. Pru had given Roy hell for that. Seeing someone else on the receiving end of Pru's temper was kind of nice for a change.

But Brice hadn't really expected her to…rescue him, he realized. After all, she was a Randolph. She probably did it because he'd shushed-up his aunt Rose and cousin Myrtle when he and Pru had told *his* family about the marriage. He hadn't expected he'd do that. Then again, he couldn't believe his family—except for his mother, of course, who was far more concerned about the condition of her new carpet—thought Pru would actually brainwash him into marriage. They even suspected she'd drugged him so he'd propose to her. Or that she knew some deep dark secret about him and was blackmailing him into marriage. Did they really think she was that desperate for a husband? A woman who looked like Pru wouldn't have to force anyone to marry her. Maybe his family did need therapy.

Gee, this marriage was off to a terrific start. The feud was worse instead of better. Their families where madder than wet cats at both of them, and they were stuck with each other when they were more used to arguing like cowpokes on a Friday night than simply talking. That's exactly why there couldn't be a marriage, no matter what Judge Willis had decreed.

Brice left his coat and cummerbund—who in the hell had invented that instrument of torture?—in the truck and crept up close to the house. He wouldn't have worn a tux at all, but he didn't want the stuffy Randolphs to think he didn't know how to dress for the occasion.

The sun had dipped to the other side of the house where all the activity was, leaving the back in the shadows. The last time he'd talked to Pru, she'd been leaving for the Willises'. Sunny Willis was helping Pru get ready for the big event, something she was looking forward to about as much as he was. Maybe if they talked one more time face-to-face, they could come up with some last-minute save. The trick was to talk to Pru alone. The deliriously happy couple couldn't very well discuss ways of ending their marriage in public or on a phone, where anyone could listen in—and in Serenity everyone listened in to everything.

As Brice inched along the flower beds, he took care not to trample Sunny's blue and pink pansies and yellow and white daffodils. Her gardens were legendary. He heard voices coming from an open window by the rose arbor bedecked with deep pink rosebuds. It was Sunny's voice.

Flattening himself against the side of the house, Brice craned his neck and peeked inside. Pru sat on a stool in the middle of the bedroom, staring straight ahead. To the clueless, she might seem lost in love or just sublimely happy. Brice knew it was really heart-stopping terror, because he felt the same way. Sunny was fussing about Pru like a mamma robin around her hatchling.

When Sunny said she was going to get a steam iron to touch up a few wrinkles in Pru's wedding dress, Brice knew this was his chance. He waited for the door to click shut, then he tapped on the screen. "Psst. Pru. Out here."

Prudence jerked alert. "Brice?" She came over to the window and gripped the curtain. Desperation covered her face. "You came to tell me you thought of a way out of this, didn't you?"

"Actually, I came to see if *you* thought of anything."

"For heaven's sake, you're the fast-riding, sure-roping cowboy. You think of something."

"What the hell does riding and roping have to do with getting out of a marriage?"

"I don't know." She gave a big sigh that seemed to come all the way from her toes and made her shoulders slouch.

Pru never had slouching shoulders. Brice felt a little sorry for her, though not as sorry as he felt for himself, of course. Then he noticed that her shoulders happened to be...bare. She wore a long white slip that shimmered when she moved, outlined the fullness of her cleavage and skimmed over her hips. How could he have known Pru for twenty-eight years and not noticed these things? Even through the screen he could tell she had skin that glistened like early-morning dew. Her hair was done up in long curls that made her blue eyes seem even larger than usual. She might have been nervous and tense, even discouraged, but she smelled of springtime, wild flowers and warm vanilla.

To hell with vanilla wafers and pound cake. Right now, Brice wanted nothing more than to nibble Pru's shoulder, her creamy neck and all her other lovely vanilla body parts. He was totally turned on by the woman he was about to marry but didn't want to marry and who certainly didn't want to marry him. How could a marriage be so damn confusing?

She said, "You do realize that if we get married today we'll have to stay that way until Willis comes to his senses and sees this idiotic marriage idea is only making the feud worse. If we even hint at a divorce before Willis caves in, things will go straight to hell in a handbasket. My family will say it's your fault, your family will say it's mine. I'm not good enough for you, you're not good enough for me. The families will do more battle, and Willis will say it's our fault and go crazy as a cuckoo bird, and Randolphs and McCormacks will all wind up behind bars before the Fourth of July. It's either figure a way out of this marriage now, or we're married till Willis realizes his plan isn't worth sheep dip. Which it isn't. At all." She raised her arms to the ceiling. "We're doomed, Brice. Totally doomed."

And he was totally doomed, because Pru had the nicest breasts and sexiest shape he'd ever laid eyes on. "Maybe Willis will come around faster than we think." And it would have to be mighty quick, too, because if Brice got excited just standing in front of a window looking at Pru, what would happen when they lived together?

Nothing, that's what. Because a marriage couldn't change the hostility between him and Pru on a family level or on a personal one. The only answer was to end this blasted marriage before it began.

Pru suddenly turned away from him, flattened her back to the window, and said, "Sunny, you're back. That didn't take long."

Sunny laughed. It was a sound that suited her name perfectly and was in direct contrast to Brice's mood. She said, "A little steaming on that beautiful dress of yours made those wrinkles come right out. Lucky for you, Brenda's Bridal Boutique had a dress that was to your liking and only needed to be hemmed and tucked a bit."

"Thank you for being my matron of honor and pulling together this wedding so fast."

Brice moved away from the window. So much commotion over a wedding that neither the bride nor groom wanted. He crept out of the flower garden, then retrieved his coat and cummerbund from the front seat of his truck. On second thought, he tossed the cummerbund back. Marrying was one thing he had to do, but he didn't have to do it wrapped like a sausage. Think, man, think! How can this wedding be stopped?

He could hear cars pulling into the driveway as he rounded the side of the picture-perfect ranch house complete with wide front porches, an old wood swing and blooming forsythias, redbuds and dogwoods. All the work trucks were gone, and large white baskets of flowers now lined the driveway. Leading the way to the tent where the ceremony would take place were lattice arches covered with ivy.

How had Sunny and her husband pulled this shindig together in three days? Incredible. Then again, Brice knew all too well that when Judge Willis set his mind to something, it happened. Nothing and no one got in his way.

Brice decided that staying hidden in the shadows of the house until the wedding began was a good idea, because his arrival would be like gasoline thrown on a smoldering fire. He watched McCormacks and Randolphs walk through the arches and take seats in the tent. He and Pru had agreed not to involve any other family in the marriage, except for Brice's having his brother as best man. That would keep confrontations to a minimum. Maybe.

The custom of families sitting on opposite sides during the wedding was convenient; it would help keep peace during the ceremony. The reception, where people mixed and mingled, would be another story. Brice intended to make this the shortest, fastest reception in Texas history—cut cake, eat cake, go home.

Out of the corner of his eye he caught sight of his mother, dressed in her favorite colors of pale blue and yellow, and Derek getting out of his new Bronco. As always, Mamma was an ace at rolling with the punches, and would wish him well if he'd chosen to marry Attila the Hun—as long as Attila didn't muddy up her house or try to run off with her secret apple butter recipe. Mamma was a homemaker of the first order, ran the McCormack house with expert precision and always had complete confidence in Brice to do what was right for the family and the ranch. Her confidence in him was unfailing, just as was his confidence in her, and he was eternally grateful for her not questioning him now when he needed her support the most.

Younger brothers were also great to have around in times of crisis, Brice decided as he watched Derek take his mother's arm. They would do stuff for you, like dress up in uncomfortable clothes and be your best man without asking a million questions. And on top of it all, they considered it all a huge honor.

Brice watched Derek escort their mother into the tent, then come back outside, obviously looking for him. He stepped out of the shadows, and Derek jogged over.

"Hey, brother. How you holding up? You're looking calm enough, which means you're in a mighty big panic."

"Thanks for the observation."

Derek grinned. "Not every day a McCormack marries a Randolph."

"You're enjoying seeing me sweat, aren't you."

Derek's grin broadened, and he stuffed his hands into the pants pockets. He wore a tux well. Derek wore everything well. Every female in Serenity would readily attest to that. Derek rocked back on his heels and said, "Good to see *you* sweating over a woman for a change, instead of me. I bet right now hearts all over Texas are busting wide open 'cause Brice McCormack's being taken off the market."

"I wasn't involved with that many hearts."

Derek arched his brow. "Why that's a damn shame, brother of mine. But the Half-Circle and family can do that to a guy—keep him too busy for anything else." Derek winked. "'Cept me, of course." Derek's grin grew. "But then, I'm not head honcho of everything McCormack like you are. Personally, I'd rather direct my attentions to the idea of 'so many women, so little time' than the idea of profit and loss."

Brice shook his head. "Cattlemen and farmers, lock up your womenfolk. Derek McCormack's on the loose."

"Damn straight."

Some small part of Brice could remember when he felt that way, too. When his father was in charge and the Half-Circle was his to run and worry over. But that was a lifetime ago, before Dad died, before his uncles had young families and couldn't manage a growing spread and oil business to boot, before he'd taken over the lion's share of work and family responsibilities.

That's why deep down, he'd pretty much accepted the fact that marriage was out. No woman would understand the constant family demands made on him...except...Pru. Now, that was an interesting thought.

"Go find Willis and help him keep a lid on this place till Pru and I get this marriage done and over with, okay?"

Derek gave Brice a questioning look. "Done and over with? You sure are anxious to tie the knot." A little twinkle sparked in Derek's eyes. "Then again, Prudence is a mighty fine-looking gal, Randolph or not. I can see why you just couldn't keep your hands off a pretty little package like that."

Brice's insides clenched, remembering just how pretty a package Pru really was. Of course, that didn't matter to him. Eventually Willis would wise up and see the marriage idea was bad. Then he and Pru could slowly and carefully dissolve their marriage so as not to cause more Randolph-McCormack discord, and everything would go back to the way it had been for the past seventy years.

For the moment, Derek seemed to be content to just stare at Brice, enjoying his misery. "Can you get a move on, little brother? Make yourself useful as well as ornamental?"

"Don't go snorting around like a bull at breeding time. You got all your life to spend with Prudence. I gotta tell you, though, never in a million years would I have expected you two to get hitched, the way you're always snarling around each other. Fact is, it sometimes seemed that Prudence would go out of her way to pick a fight with you. Never would have guessed it to be a smoke screen for true love."

"Yeah, nothing but a big smoke screen." So it

wasn't just his imagination; Pru *was* more prickly with him than the other McCormacks. Strange.

Derek sucker-punched Brice on the arm. ''Relax, will you? Lighten up. Forget about the Half-Circle and the family for a while. It's your wedding day.'' Derek laughed deep in his chest and turned toward the tent. After a few steps he called over his shoulder, ''And I'm sure as hell glad it's yours and not mine.''

Brice heaved a sigh as he edged back into the shadows, but he didn't move quite fast enough. Pru's dad was heading his way at a fast clip. Oh, yeah, talking to Bob Randolph was just what Brice wanted to do right now. Gee, he could hardly wait.

Bob Randolph was a big man, and looked perpetually gruff in his usual bank attire of dark suit and board-starched white shirt. Today he looked gruffer than usual, if that were possible. His wife had died when Pru was ten, and he'd never remarried. Too bad, because if he had he might have focused on something else aside from pushing Pru into doing this and that and some other thing.

Brice had often wondered just whose idea it was for artsy-fartsy Prudence Randolph to go to law school. Hers, or that of a father who wanted an attorney in the family to help run the businesses? Either way, it had worked out. Being an attorney suited Pru. Heaven knows, she was good enough at it—he had battle scars to prove it.

''McCormack,'' Bob Randolph said as he drew up in front of Brice, meeting him eyeball to eyeball. ''I don't know what the hell's going on between you and my daughter, but I don't much like it. I tried to talk some sense into her for the past three days and get her to call off this damn wedding, but she's downright bullheaded about marrying you. Can't believe she's bucking me on this—that's not like Prudence at all.'' For a moment he looked completely dumbfounded. ''Blast it all! Nothing about this marriage makes an ant's ear full of sense, since Prudence never seemed to even *like* you in the first place.''

''Look, Randolph, Prudence and I are in—''

Bob Randolph sliced his hand through the air, cutting Brice off. ''I don't want to hear that poppycock about being in love. My daughter's not in love with you. For criminy's sake, man, you're a McCormack! Prudence has just gone plumb loco, that's all. Must be one of those female things. There's no other explanation. But I'm telling you now, if I hear you're not treating my girl right, you and I are going to tangle. Get my drift?'' He poked Brice hard in the chest with his forefinger to emphasize every word, then he turned and left.

Under normal circumstances, Brice didn't take lightly to being threatened—especially by a Randolph—and he usually did something to remind the offender this was not a good idea. But nothing about this day was normal. And there was something else, too. Brice had to admit that if the tables were turned, if it were *his* daughter marrying someone he didn't approve of, Brice would be doing the same thing Bob Randolph had just done. Realizing he and Bob Randolph actually agreed on something was unsettling as hell.

Organ music now drifted out from the tent, and Brice watched Judge Willis take his place in the front; he was flanked by Derek and by Sunny, who was holding a bouquet of lilacs and daffodils large enough to conceal the state of Rhode Island. A four-tiered cake—Brice's two vanilla layers, Pru's two chocolate—was perched on a table in the corner. For the moment, everything was calm, very wedding-like. Even the afternoon sun peeking over the white fluff of clouds and the breeze ruffling the tree tops now pale green with new leaves seemed to be a good omen.

The tension in Brice's shoulders eased a bit, and he relaxed—just as screams erupted from the tent. Brice turned to see fists flying and people and chairs scattering everywhere.

Chapter Three

"Holy hell! Stop!" Brice yelled, entering the tent. Two flower baskets toppled as Derek lit into a Randolph who was giving as good as he got. A fist came out of nowhere, striking Brice in the eye. Reflexes took over and Brice struck back, knocking a Randolph into Judge Willis, sending them both onto the ground, narrowly missing the cake. For once, the judge seemed dazed and speechless. Too bad that hadn't happened three days ago when he'd dreamed up this madness.

Another fist connected with Brice's jaw, and Brice's fist connected with a Randolph nose. Whatever made the judge think a wedding would bring the families together?

"That's enough!" Pru's voice carried over the mayhem. "Stop it! Stop it, all of you right now. This is my wedding day, and I won't have you all fighting and ruining everything."

When Brice looked around, to his amazement he saw that everyone had done as she said. Then he gazed at Pru and realized why.

She was the most beautiful bride he'd ever seen. Unlike the tailored, buttoned-up attorney he clashed with in Judge Willis's court, this Prudence was fresh as spring and all done up in flowing white silk, delicate lace and satin ribbons. This was, indeed, her wedding day, and that one fact seemed to matter more to everyone in the tent than fighting, at least for the moment.

That was good, and that was bad. Good in that no one was fighting. Bad in that it gave Judge Willis a speck of validation his plan would work, dashing any hope Brice had that this marriage would not happen. Since the unexpected moratorium wouldn't last, *now* was the time to get the deed done.

Brice caught the eye of the frazzled organist, who once again started the music, only messing up a few dozen notes. He nervously nodded to Derek, Sunny and Judge Willis, and they reclaimed their positions in the front of the tent. The congregation kept their places, taking in the event as if they couldn't believe what was happening.

Pru must have felt the same way when she heard the fight break out, because she didn't have her bouquet or veil. Hell, she didn't even have shoes. Brice could see her stocking feet peeking out from under the folds of her dress. Her toenails were painted hot pink. She had really cute piggies. He snatched a handful of pansies and daffodils from one of the overturned baskets, shook off the water and handed them to her.

Their gazes locked, and for a second they seemed

to reach an understanding. This was not a marriage made in heaven but a marriage of necessity to keep their families safe, and the one thing they agreed on was that family was everything.

Quickly taking his place by Derek, Brice straightened his collar, smoothed back his hair the best he could, felt his eye begin to swell shut, and waited for his bride to walk down the aisle…or what was left of it, toward him.

PRUDENCE FELT THE GRASS tickle her toes as she walked toward Brice. Holy samoli. She was marrying Brice McCormack, rancher, oilman, thief of lands not belonging to him, and personal opponent.

Today he had a split lip, an eye that was beginning to purple, and a squashed blue pansy stuck to the leg of his black pants. His hair was mussed and falling over his forehead, and she noticed his hand was red and swollen. Except for the pansy, he looked completely disreputable, and had to be the least likely person to ever fit into her life. She'd heard somewhere that if you wanted to make God laugh, tell him your plans. Well, God must be laughing his behind off right about now.

She never thought she would do the walk down the aisle thing. She didn't have time for marriage. Couldn't possibly accommodate another person, especially a male, in her life. Keeping up with the expectations of her dad and family was exhausting enough.

Brice discreetly hooked his finger at her and

hitched his chin, suggesting she hurry up. Good grief, not only did she have to marry the man, she had to set a speed-wedding record doing it. She quickened her pace, keeping it just under a jog. This was *not* a Martha Stewart wedding.

The moment Prudence reached the front of the tent, Brice stood beside her. They faced the judge, who was already beyond the "we are gathered here" part of the ceremony and on to the "with this ring" part. The "does anyone object" part had already been addressed, and obviously Judge Willis had decided not to visit that particular passage again.

Brice snatched the simple gold rings from Derek's palm. After Pru handed her fistful of flowers to Sunny, Brice slipped a band on Pru's finger, as she did the same to him. A heartbeat later Judge Willis declared, "I now pronounce you man and wife."

It was done. Prudence could hardly believe that after seventy years of doing battle, a McCormack and a Randolph were officially—for better or for worse, depending on your point of view—married.

A funeral-like pall filled the tent. Judge Willis broke the hush with "Brice, you may now kiss the bride." The congregation stirred as if awakening from a trance. Kiss? Prudence felt her heart stop and her eyes widen. She stared straight ahead. With all the other parts of the ceremony to worry about, she'd forgotten about the "you may kiss" part. Not only did she have to kiss a McCormack, but she also had to look as if it was a good thing, even great. How was she going to pull this off?

Brice's strong, decisive fingers captured her chin and turned her face toward his. Her gaze went from the determined set of his bruised jaw, to his cut lip, to his eyes—one puffy, one chocolate brown. She caught a flicker of uncertainty in it, just as his mouth claimed hers.

She gasped in surprise at his soft, gentle kiss. Of course, anything else would have hurt him like the dickens. Then she realized his lips were also warm, inviting, very seductive. The callused pad of Brice's thumb traced the length of her throat, and his hand tenderly cupped the back of her head as if laying claim to what he held. Her heart started to pound like the drumbeat at a parade and her blood began to flow like warm honey on hot breakfast toast. A fiery ache burned deep inside her.

From somewhere far off, Prudence heard Judge Willis order everyone to plant themselves right where they were and not move an inch. That was just fine with her. She had no intention of going anywhere; Brice not only kissed like a dream, but smelled of deep-forest pine and tasted like something delicious…even addicting.

She held on to him for support because this whole experience had caught her completely off guard, making her as dizzy and confused as a duck hit on the head.

"I said no fighting!" Judge Willis yelled. Then a gunshot split the air. Prudence jumped back, as screams filled the tent. The second round of fist-throwing stopped before it really got started, and everyone stood as if glued where they stood. There had definitely been enough fighting and enough kissing for one day. The altercations she'd expected; kissing Brice, and her reaction to his kisses, were completely bewildering. She didn't look at him. She couldn't, or she just might kiss him again.

Gads, her brain was not working at all. Brice was the enemy. Why couldn't she remember that one little fact that had ruled her entire life? Kissing him should have been a dreadful experience.

"Jumpin' Jehoshaphat," the judge said as he stood on a chair, holding a smoking revolver pointed straight up over his head. "I'm fed up with this foolishness from all Randolphs and McCormacks!" A small, round shaft of afternoon sunlight peeked through a new hole in the top of the tent.

The judge glared, then said, "The next person who dares to throw a punch in this here tent is spending the night in jail, and that's a promise. Do you all hear me? This wedding's over. Brice and Prudence are married. I'd advise you all to get used to it. I want everyone to leave here nice and peaceful-like, and I'll keep standing up here to make sure you do. Prudence and Brice will cut the cake and hand you a piece as you go. And if there's a hint of trouble, I'm putting in a call to Sheriff Pritchard. Everybody get the picture?"

A HALF-HOUR LATER, Prudence licked icing from her thumb and put down the cake knife, as she, Brice, the judge and Sunny watched the last car roll out of the driveway.

"See," said the judge as he climbed down from his perch on the folding chair, "you two got hitched and everything's just fine as frog's hair."

Prudence choked. "Fine? You call a brawl and gunshots fine?"

She watched Brice put down the ice pack he'd used to nurse his eye and pick up the cake knife. He cut himself a hefty piece of the white layer of the cake, plopping a vanilla butter-cream rose on top. Pure lust gleamed in his one good eye. Hmm, Brice McCormack, rough-and-tumble rancher, headstrong attorney and fist fighter had a passion for things vanilla? Who would have thought?

Judge Willis loosened his black string tie complete with ornate silver slide and ends. He grinned as an early-evening breeze kicked up, ruffling his thinning hair—hair that looked grayer than it had yesterday. He said, "Why, this here was a great wedding. No one had to be rushed to the emergency room, did they? There were no broken bones, no bloodshed. All in all, I'd say things went right smoothly."

Brice forked a piece of cake into his mouth and licked icing from the corners. Prudence felt her heart slam against her ribs, and she bit her bottom lip, remembering just how wonderful his mouth had felt on hers. Not that she wanted to recall that particular incident. Gee, it was hot for a spring day.

"Judge," Brice said, dragging Prudence back to the present. "A smooth wedding is when people toss rice, not punches, and they laugh and eat and dance merrily about. *Not* where the judge has a gun sticking out of the waistband of his pants.'' Brice eyed the pearl handle of a Colt Peacemaker resting over the judge's belt buckle. He glanced at Sunny's large bouquet, now sitting on a folding chair. ''Sunny had the gun hidden in her bouquet, didn't she.''

Sunny smoothed the skirt of her lavender suit, a perfect accent to her silver hair. ''Well, you see,'' she said in a lovely Texas drawl, ''in case things got out of hand, the judge and I decided there might be a need to get people's attention right quick-like. His granddaddy's Peacemaker makes a powerful noise, so it seemed the logical choice. But don't you and Prudence bother yourselves with such things. In no time this nasty old feud will just be a part of Serenity's colorful history. You're such a precious couple, I'm sure everyone will get used to you being married in no time at all.''

''Don't know about that,'' Brice said. ''Pru and I can't even get used to it.''

He bit into another big piece of cake, and more icing caught on his lips. Prudence looked away. If he licked it off she'd melt, she was sure of it.

The judge scoffed. ''From the looks of the way you two played kissy-face, I think you've got the hang of this marriage business.''

''All for show,'' Brice said around a mouthful. ''If you want us married, we have to look the part.''

Prudence cringed. That kiss that had rocked her to her stocking-covered toes and was giving her severe aftershocks was just for show? It hadn't affected Brice one bit?

That no good rattlesnake!

She should have expected as much from Brice McCormack. Everyone knew the only things that stirred the man's blood were cows and oil wells—definitely not a Randolph. That was just fine and dandy with her. It would make steering clear of him until Willis called off this stupid marriage as easy as swatting a fly.

The judge pointed down the drive. "Isn't that John Pritchard's cruiser heading our way? Wonder what the sheriff wants."

Brice dusted crumbs from his hands. "Probably here to snatch a piece of wedding cake."

They watched the cruiser pull to a stop and the sheriff unfold his lanky frame from behind the wheel. Pritchard settled his hat on his head, hitched up his belt and ambled over to the tent.

"Howdy, John," said the judge. "What brings you out to these parts? Come to congratulate Brice and Prudence on their nuptials?"

"Not exactly." The sheriff tipped his hat to everyone, then rested it on the back of his head. He let out a sigh, the kind that sounded as if it had been building all day.

Judge Willis nodded and grinned. "Wedding went off without a hitch—well, maybe a little hitch, but I knew once we got the Randolphs and McCormacks together things would settle down. I was right."

"Not exactly." Sheriff Pritchard took a toothpick

from his breast pocket and rested the pick in the corner of his mouth.

Judge Willis's enthusiasm dimmed. "What're you getting at, John?"

The toothpick anchored itself to the sheriff's lips as he said, "Seems a bunch of the McCormack and Randolph men decided to drown their problems over at the Powder Keg. Didn't take long for all hell to break loose." He eyed the overturned folding chairs and squashed flowers. "Looks like things didn't fare any better here." He looked back to the judge. "Anyways, right now I got myself three Randolphs occupying one cell and four McCormacks in the other. And I got a bill here for five-hundred dollars in barroom damages that's got to get paid, or the owner is going to file charges."

He handed both Brice and Prudence a tally, then continued. "I'm thinking the two of you best come on into town and straighten out your kin. 'Course, you could let the lot of 'em cool their heels in the pokey overnight. That might be just the ticket to get them to think before they take a swing."

Tension and fatigue felt like a hundred-pound weight strapped to Prudence's back. This day was as long as a week, she was sure of it. The sun just forgot to set a couple of times. "Give me a few minutes to change."

"I'm coming," Brice said, suddenly looking as tired as she felt.

"Well, hell's bells," said the judge, running his

hand through his hair. "Thought we were done with fistfights for one day."

"Not exactly." The sheriff hooked his thumbs over his belt. "As I see it, this here marriage is going to do one of two things. Either the McCormacks and Randolphs are going to start getting along, or the feuding's going to get worse than ever." He stared at Brice, then Prudence; he worked his toothpick. "'Fraid my money's on things getting worse. Hope you two know what you're getting yourselves into."

THE MOON HUNG LOW in the eastern sky as Brice waited on the front steps of the courthouse for Pru to finish talking to her two uncles and her cousin. The seven McCormack-Randolph jailbirds had been given hefty fines and ordered to paint the bleachers at the high school football field. Judge Willis was in a lousy mood. In fact, everyone in Serenity was in a lousy mood tonight, except the town gossips. The past couple of days had to be the motherlode of local dirt for them.

From the look on Pru's face right now and the bits and pieces of conversation drifting his way, Brice figured she was giving her relatives the same lecture he'd just delivered to his—go home, stay out of trouble and *leave us alone.*

Brice touched the corner of his left eye, testing the discomfort level. Right now it was registering about four on the *ouch* scale. His lip had diminished to a three. This was the best he'd felt in the past few hours, *except* for when he'd kissed Pru. Kissing her had been unexpected ecstasy.

When she'd parted her lips and his tongue had grazed hers for only a second, he'd never felt better in his life. In spite of the pandemonium it would have caused, he'd felt an almost uncontrollable urge to make love to her right there in the middle of a Randolph-McCormack fistfight, surrounded by screaming ladies and overturned flowerpots.

Blast it all! Why did he feel this way? He and Pru weren't in love. They weren't even in like. How could Brice even be attracted to Pru? Then he looked at her, standing on the courthouse steps, and knew the answer to his own question. She had a great body, sexy-as-hell lips, and an energy and confidence that intrigued him more than that of any other woman he'd ever met.

Brice gave himself a mental shake. He'd just have to ignore Prudence Randolph's desirable attributes—he'd ignored them for the past twenty-eight years, hadn't he?—and concentrate on the aspects of Pru that drove him nuts. Then they could get through this marriage business till Willis realized the error of his ways, and they could part company and forget this marriage ever happened.

"Well," Brice said, when Pru came his way. They were the only two left on the courthouse steps, and a single overhead lamp swung gently to and fro, casting shadows against the columns. "You have any suggestions what we should do tonight?"

Very deep sigh. ''Run away, change our names to Smith and join the French Foreign Legion?''

He felt a grin coming on. ''We'd never make it over the county line before old Willis would drag our sorry butts back. Leaving our families alone right now would turn Serenity into a first-class war zone.'' He raked his hand through his hair. ''I suppose we should scrap our honeymoon plans.''

Pru gasped. ''No honeymoon? Not that!'' She put her palms to her cheeks and shook her head. ''I was so looking forward to the cattle auction in Amarillo. Woe is me.''

He folded his arms. ''Hey, I can't help it if I had that auction planned for months. I need a bull.''

A devilish smile rippled across her face. It unnerved him when he saw Pru like that. It was as if he got a glimpse of some part of her that he didn't know at all.

She said, ''It seems to me, cowboy, there's already more than enough bull at the Half-Circle.''

''Cute.''

''Couldn't resist.'' She planted her hands on her hips. ''You do know the McCormacks threw the first punch in this little altercation over at the Powder Keg tonight, don't you?''

''Cripes, Pru.'' His grin faded, right along with hers. It was back to business as usual. ''Only after your uncle Roy pushed Granddad off his bar stool. That was a heck of a thing to do.''

Her eyes widened. ''Is that what Wes told you?

Ha! He was so inebriated, he fell off that stool. He's trying to blame—''

Brice threw his hands in the air. ''All right, all right, all right. I'm not into arguing with you right now. It's going on midnight, and I'm too dog-tired to fight about our families.'' Was this lawyer-woman really the sweet, innocent-looking, barefoot bride who'd walked down the aisle to marry him? The one who nearly knocked him off his feet with one kiss? What had happened to transform her back into the attorney from hell?

Defending the Randolphs—that's what had happened. Then again, defending the McCormacks didn't exactly turn him into Mr. Wonderful. Their first allegiance was, and always would be, to their families, and that didn't leave room for much compromise between the two of them.

''We can spend the night at the River's Edge Inn—it's just around the corner.''

Pru's slacks and blouse were mussed, and her fancy wedding hairdo had been reduced to a mass of auburn springs. He'd never realized her hair was so...lively, since she always wore it pinned up or pulled back. Who would have thought someone so perfectly neat and organized had hair that was anything but.

Pru said, ''If we go to the inn, we'll have to ask for two rooms.''

She shook her head, freeing a few more strands to curl around her face. Damn, he liked her hair.

She continued. ''It would take about ten minutes

for that tasty little morsel to get dished all over town, and our cover as the lovey-dovey couple would be blown. Willis would never believe it was an accident, and things would be worse than ever. We'll spend the night at my apartment—you get the couch."

"But—"

"And I've been thinking about where we should live. Twin Pines has some great condos. In the morning we can look for a permanent residence there."

Pru started down the stairs, but Brice caught her arm, turning her toward him. "Hold on there just a minute, city girl."

"Now what?"

"For openers, I'm not spending the night at your place, connected to your dad's house and next to your uncle Roy's. I like my head and other vital body parts attached where they are, thank you. And," he rushed on before Pru could interrupt, "what made you think we're going to live in town in some damn condo?"

She wrinkled her nose, looking confused. "Of course we're living in town. I've always lived in town. And in case you forgot, that's where I work. Town it is."

"In case *you* forgot, I run the Half-Circle. I can't live here, especially in a condo." The thought of such a confined place made his stomach turn. "How does anyone survive in those damn little boxes that all look alike, anyway?"

She put her nose to within an inch of his. That was as tall as her tiptoes would make her. Her breath warmed his lips, and her eyes danced in the moonlight. Pru was one damn attractive female, but he still wasn't living in any pigeonhole condo.

"Apartments and condos are great," she said. "And as for the Half-Circle, you can drive there in your macho black truck. That's what roads are for. If there's a problem, heaven knows there are lots and lots of McCormacks around the ranch to handle things. And," she added, "hear this, cowboy, I may have had to marry a McCormack, but I'm not living on McCormack land, *ever.*"

"Tell you what, we'll just solve this the democratic way—we'll flip to see where we stay." He pulled his fifty-cent piece from the watch pocket of his jeans, then tossed it in the air, calling "heads" before Pru could object. "Gee, Pru," he said as he gazed at the coin in his palm, "it's—"

"I don't give a rat's behind what that coin says, I'm not living in a ranch house, and definitely not a *McCormack* ranch house."

She looked tired but full of fight. Could this day get any worse? "You're a McCormack now, don't forget."

Fire blazed in her eyes. Hmm, guess that wasn't the best thing to say. Her face took on a purple-red hue. She was going to pop something if she wasn't careful. She tried to speak but words refused to come out.

"Ah!" she finally managed to say. "Like I *want* to be a McCormack? That name is yours, and you can keep and put it—"

"Got a piece of paper and a pen in your purse?"

"What in the world for?"

He gave her an exasperated look. "Do you or not?"

"Good grief," she mumbled, then snapped open her bag. "I've got a pen." She held it up.

Brice searched his pockets, locating a scrap of paper.

"What's that?"

He tilted it up to the dim light. "Looks like a receipt for Big Al's Buffalo Wings." He looked closer. "Double order. Extra spicy. Side order of chili fries with cheese and a large soda. Sounds mighty tasty about now."

Prudence huffed. "What in blue blazes do buffalo wings have to do with all this? And," she added, nodding at the paper, "I can't believe you really ate all that and lived."

"That's man's food."

"No wonder women live longer."

He snatched the pen from Prudence's fingers, turned the receipt over and held it against one of the wood columns. Then he wrote.

He could feel her gaze on him. More times than not he could feel when she was looking at him or even when she walked into a room. Must be some sixth sense from being in each other's hair for so damn long.

She asked, "What are you doing? We have a problem here that's not going to be settled over buffalo wings—that much I can tell you."

"Just hold your horses a second, will you?" He

wrote a few more lines, then handed it to her. ''Here—'' he said. ''Now you don't have to worry about living in a 'McCormack' ranch house. There's a new barn and a farm house on some property we bought last fall. It added land to our west range, where I intend to raise some stock on strictly organic grains. Anyway, the place is about five miles outside of town.'' He nodded at the paper in her hand. ''I just deeded you the house. It's yours, for as long as we're married. *Now* will you agree to live in it?''

She stared at the paper, then at Brice, then back at the paper. ''You gave me a house?''

''Yeah, city girl, I gave you a house, a ranch house. The old Dillard place. It's yours.''

''You really gave me a house?''

Her eyes were so big and blue. Even in the dim light he could see their clear, bright color that reminded him of a Texas summer sky. A twinge of guilt that he tried to ignore rippled across his shoulders. He had to stay on the Half-Circle, no matter what it took. No one knew the operation the way he did, and everyone depended on him. ''So, can we go now, or what?''

She looked a little less tired, and Brice's guilty twinge felt more like a quake when she said, ''We have to live somewhere—guess it might as well be in my...house. I never had a house of my own before.'' She skipped down the steps, heading for her Lincoln parked at the curb. She called over her shoulder, ''Did you decorate the place yourself or have someone do it for you?''

Decorate? Maybe he shouldn't have called it a house. Maybe he should have said...cottage. Yeah, *cottage* would have been better. It was kind of a woodsy place, as he remembered from when he and his new cow pony had bunked down there in the rain storms and cold weather. Couldn't leave his horse in a leaky barn now, could he? Then he recalled how the house hadn't been much better. 'Course, he'd built a new barn since then, but the house—

"Does it have a nice yard?" Pru asked, sounding much too cheery for Brice's peace of mind. "I haven't seen the Dillard place since I was a kid." She stopped by his truck and looked up at him, then smiled.

Aw, hell! Did she have to smile? Brice ambled down the steps. "The house is hard to find at night. The road's not in the best of shape. I'll drive us out. We can stop by the Willises' and get your things on the way, then pick your car up tomorrow."

As he helped Pru into the truck, he decided he should have called the place a cabin. *Cabin* would have been much better. Sandbagging his new wife on her wedding night wasn't a very nice thing to do, even if she was a Randolph. Besides, there was also the possibility that once Pru saw the...house... cottage...cabin, she might strangle Brice with her bare hands.

Married life had some mighty serious pitfalls, especially if the marriage was between a Randolph and a McCormack. Brice had the unsettling feeling that this was to be the first of many.

Chapter Four

Prudence held on to the dashboard of Brice's pickup and tried to steady herself, as it bounced into another pothole. "Jeez, where is this house of mine, anyway?"

"We're almost there."

The truck lurched again, making her head snap back as if it were spring-mounted and her hand slip, landing on Brice's thigh. His firm leg muscles flexed under her fingers. His body heat radiated through his worn-smooth jeans, instantly warming her from the tips of her fingers to the ends of her toes. She glanced at him out of the corner of her eye as she slid her hand away.

How could just touching Brice make her feel so...hot? Something was wrong with the truck, like a malfunctioning heating system, she decided, because she certainly wasn't that enamored with Brice. So he was a great kisser. Lots of guys were great kissers. And the fact they were married didn't change that he was her arch enemy. He was still the very same person her father had always compared her to, the one person she never quite measured up to, the one person she had prayed would run away from home and leave her in peace. She refused to be attracted to Brice McCormack now or ever, married or not.

The truck lurched again, and this time she kept her hand on the seat. "Well, you're right about one thing—my Lincoln would never make it up this road."

"This isn't exactly a road. It's what's called a two-track 'cause it's only wide enough for one wagon leaving two tracks in the dirt." Low branches swished across the windshield, momentarily plunging them into darkness, cutting them off from the illumination of the headlights. "You should get a truck. Something with four-wheel drive. Lincoln's a sissy car, anyway."

"Hey, watch that sissy stuff. My Town Car has spunk, grit and fights rush hour with uncommon valor. The Lincoln stays."

"Pru." He glanced sideways at her. "Look around. This ain't town."

He had a point. "So this house, is sort of...rustic, then?"

"Rustic? You could call it rustic."

Prudence watched Brice for a moment. He looked tense, even edgy, and seemed to be getting edgier by the minute. But it had been that kind of day. How many grooms got a split lip and black eye at their own wedding, then had to bail their kin out of jail after the ceremony? Brice would feel better once they got to the house, she was sure of it.

''Dark as sin out here.'' She hadn't seen a street or traffic light or any kind of light anywhere since they'd left town.

''Look up.'' Brice pointed outside.

''Where? It's all black.''

Big sigh. ''Just look up, will you.''

She gave an indignant sniff, pressed her nose to the glass and peered into the darkness...and the moonlight. She'd seen moonlight before, of course, but out here it was...brighter...bigger. There were stars, lots and lots of them, winking at her between the clouds. Was that the Big Dipper? Maybe it was the Little Dipper. It was some kind of dipper, and it was really nice and all, but she'd give a week's salary for the glow of fluorescent and neon that meant civilization was close.

''You know,'' she said, ''living out here's going to take some getting used to.''

Unexpectedly, he took her hand, squeezing her fingers hard but not enough to hurt. ''I want you to try—really, really try—and remember that.''

Remember? The only thing she could remember at the moment was that Brice was holding her hand. His grip was strong, his palm rough and capable, his touch...memorable. Drat! She didn't need memorable.

''Here we are,'' Brice said.

Good grief, she hadn't even realized the truck had stopped. The headlights silhouetted a large tree, a line of broken fence and the side of some kind of dilapidated outbuilding.

"Well, the fence needs work," she said, "but the tree's nice." He held her hand tighter. She hoped for an attack of amnesia. "That barn thing is really a wreck. I'm surprised you'd put those prize McCormack cattle you raise in a place like that."

"I wouldn't. There's a new barn over there." He hitched his chin in the opposite direction.

"You use this place for storage?"

"It can be useful in emergencies. Pru—"

"Whatever it is, it's a real eyesore. A liability. Burn it."

"B-burn it? But you haven't seen the back, and look at that wraparound porch. It has a fine porch. Missing a few steps and some floorboards, but still a great porch."

"Forget the porch." She wished she could forget Brice's hand over hers. It felt wonderful. Too wonderful. "This place will devalue your house, make that *my* house, and—"

"Pru, this *is* the house." He drew in a deep breath. "The one I just deeded to you."

Slowly she turned sideways and stared at him. She wanted to see the laughter in his one good eye that said "gotcha" because he'd pulled a joke on her. But his eye wasn't laughing. His lips weren't smiling. The man was dead serious.

"You have the nerve to call this…this pile of boards, this good excuse for a bonfire, this mess, a *house?* Even a McCormack wouldn't call this a house.''

Brice rubbed the back of his neck. ''Guess it's a little more rustic than I remembered.''

''You're a louse, Brice McCormack, you know that? A big fat, conniving louse. How could you drag me all the way out here for...for this? No wonder you deeded it to me.'' She pulled her hand from his and punched his arm, sure it hurt her more than it did him, since he didn't even flinch.

''It's like you said—it just takes a little getting used to.'' He turned off the engine.

''I was expecting the Ponderosa, Little Joe, Hoss, pretty pine trees and long lines of fences. This is just another McCormack trick to get what you want from a Randolph—to get me out here on your precious ranch so you can be close to your precious cows. No wonder Randolphs don't trust McCormacks.''

And to think that just moments ago, she'd felt all warm and fuzzy with him holding her hand. What was wrong with her? She knew better than to ever trust a McCormack. Hadn't her father drummed that into her head along with her ABCs and how to read the stock market page? There had to be some fitting retribution for Mr. Brice McCormack, like a noose hanging over a tree limb.

Prudence plopped her head against the back of her seat and closed her eyes. ''If I killed you dead, not a jury in the land would convict me.''

''Look, Pru, I have to stay at the Half-Circle. It's spring, and the ranch needs me. Things are always going haywire in the spring. I thought if you saw the house, the land, the moonlight—''

''For crying in a bucket, Brice!'' She pried open one tired eyelid and glared at him. ''There are tons of McCormack kin to run the Half-Circle.''

''*I* run the Half-Circle, Pru.''

His voice was determined and full of conviction. And deep down, she knew he was right.

''Everyone depends on me. Guess I forgot how bad this place was.'' At least he had the decency to sound contrite about that.

He continued. ''To tell you the truth, I really expected us to figure a way out of this marriage before it happened. I never gave much thought to the 'where we'd live' part of the plan, 'cause I was hoping we wouldn't make it to the 'I do' part.''

''Yeah, me, too.'' She yawned and opened both eyes. Little pinpricks of fatigue stabbed her muscles and the back of her neck. ''There are beds in there, right?'' She pointed to the house.

''Do sleeping bags count?''

She wasn't a whiner, but was giving serious consideration to converting.

''What's wrong with sleeping bags?''

''Only a McCormack would ask that question,'' she said, more to herself than to Brice. Suddenly she bolted straight up and nailed Brice with a hard look.

''What?''

''If—'' she took a deep breath, steadying her nerves, trying not to think the very worst ''—if there isn't indoor plumbing in that house, Brice McCormack, you better start running because—"

He cupped her cheeks with his hands—he really did have great hands—and gazed into her eyes.

"Now, Pru, would I give you a house that didn't have running water?"

"In a heartbeat." She pulled her face from his fingers before his touch became lethal to logical thinking. She poked Brice in the chest with her index finger, ignoring the way his soft navy shirt hugged his shoulders and fell over his flat stomach. She concentrated on her anger. "Unlike your granddaddy swindling my granddaddy, you're going to pay for this…this lie, Brice McCormack, and it sure as heck isn't going to take seventy long years. *That* you can count on."

BRICE KNEW PRU WASN'T kidding, and, if truth be told, he didn't blame her one iota for being mad. He wouldn't have pulled this stunt if he hadn't been at his wits' end.

"Come on," he said, opening the door to the truck. "Let's go inside. It's getting cold out here."

"That means the place has heat?" Pru asked with a hint of hope in her voice. Or was that just plain desperation?

Brice snatched her bag and his from the back of the truck. "The house has a fireplace. Bet you always wanted a house with a big fireplace, huh?"

"We have four fireplaces at Randolph House." He could almost hear her teeth grinding as she side-stepped mud clods and made her way over to his side of the truck. Her shoes, which were nothing more than strips of leather, wouldn't cut it out here on this ranch. But Pru in boots was a picture he couldn't conjure up.

All things considered, though, she'd been pretty good about the house business. Hey, he was still alive, wasn't he? He knew women who'd have taken care of that situation right off the bat. She hadn't burst into tears, though Pru wasn't the teary type. She was more the shoot-first-and-ask-questions-later type. And she hadn't even insisted that he take her back to town, which he'd fully expected her to do.

Then again, she hadn't seen the inside of the house. Oh, boy. Instead of pocketing the truck keys, Brice tossed them back inside the cab. They'd be easier to find that way.

"Guess grand theft auto isn't a high probability around here?"

He held Pru's arm so she wouldn't stumble in the ruts. "Well, there you are. Living in rural America has some definite advantages. You never have to go key-hunting, since you just leave them in the car. And listen to all those frogs and crickets, Pru. You don't hear them in town, now, do you?"

"Of course I do. I play my Sounds of the Deep Forest CD all the time. It has waterfalls and rain and crickets and frogs and other stuff."

Rain on demand? Nature goes platinum? She just didn't get it. He pushed open the door to the house, and the squeak of rusted hinges not wanting to budge echoed in the room.

"Where's the light switch?" Pru asked.

He could see the silhouette of her hand feeling along the wall. "Electricity's turned off. But," he rushed on so she couldn't dwell on that one little point, "we have quaint little lanterns, and there's that firepl—"

"*Brice.*"

The tone of her voice sent a chill clear up his spine, and he hadn't felt like that since a tomcat trapped him in a box canyon on the north range two years ago. "If there's no electricity, and you didn't mention a generator, that means there's no running water. You said—"

"I said there was indoor plumbing. And there is. But at the moment it's not work—" The rest of his breath rushed out in one long *whoosh* as a sharp kick landed against his shin. Little city shoes could do more harm than he'd have imagined. "Guess I had that coming." He rubbed his leg, then gingerly put his weight on it. The woman kicked like a mule.

"What in the world are we supposed to do now? We can't see worth diddly. There's no running water, no bed, no bathroom, no..."

The rest of her words faded as Brice struck a match, illuminating a small space around them. Then he took a lantern from a peg on the wall, and lit it. As the wick caught and the flame grew, a warm golden glow filled the hallway where they stood. Thank heavens, lantern light was flattering. He took a few steps into the next room and held the lantern high.

"See," Brice said, hoping the raised stone hearth in the living room would take some of the sting out of seeing worn wood floors, cracked walls and ceiling, and piles of boxes in the corner. "We have this great fireplace here, and there's lots of dry wood for us to use. This place can be fixed up. It wouldn't take any time at all."

"You're not sweet-talking me into liking this dump, cowboy. If I wasn't so tired, I'd be on my way back to Serenity—*after* I buried your sorry butt in a shallow, unmarked grave."

This might be one heck of a good time to shut his trap, Brice decided as he set the lantern on the mantel that was really a log cut lengthwise. He grabbed some saplings, dry brush and a few chunks of wood piled alongside the hearth, hunkered down and tossed them into the grate.

Prudence hadn't moved, which meant she hadn't decided to go to town, and his sorry butt was safe for the moment. If he put her to work, maybe she'd lose some of her steam. "There are matches on the mantel. If you'll light the fire, I'll find another lantern and get us some water from the well out back. It can heat up by the fire. The sleeping bags are on a shelf in what's left of the kitchen."

"What's left?"

Her tone froze him. Bad choice of words. "I mean—"

"Never mind." She exhaled a long deep breath. "I don't even want to know."

She sighed, it was a sound that suggested resignation. Hey, resignation was good, beat the heck out of her last suggestions.

She said, "I'll get the water."

He stood and looked at her in the lamplight. She was tired, tired to the bone, just the way he was. "I'll go. The bucket's heavy, and there might be spiders. I know how city girls like—"

"Brice." Her eyes darkened. "You know Pine Tree Ridge?"

He frowned. "I know where it is. Everyone does. Fact is, Sheriff caught two of my nephews over there on four-wheelers the other night, tearing up the turf. He gave 'em hell. What about it?"

"The last time I had a match in my hands, two acres there went up in flames, and I never did get my Outdoor Cook badge for scouting. Any of this ring a bell?"

"A distant one. That happened a long, long time ago, Pru."

"Same week you got your Eagle Scout badge. We both made the front page of *The Serenity Star*. Dad still has the newspaper clippings and hasn't allowed a match in our house for fifteen years. There's a message here."

Fifteen years? Hell, yes, there was a message—Bob Randolph was a jerk. Brush fires were not all that uncommon. *Forgive* and *forget* were not words in Bob Randolph's vocabulary. That didn't surprise

Brice, but he was surprised to find that it angered him. Pru had been a kid when that happened. It was an accident, and there were adults around who should have made certain everything was safe.

Brice stood and dusted his hands on his jeans. "Tell you what—we'll flip to see who gets the water." He plucked his favorite fifty-cent piece from his pocket and sent it tumbling into the air. "Heads," he called as he watched it drop onto the hearth with a clank. "Heads it is." Brice snatched up the coin and pocketed it.

Pru sounded anxious when she said, "Me and matches shouldn't be reunited on the toss of a coin, Brice. Trust me on this one."

He ignored her and took the matches from the mantel. He walked over to her and pressed them into her hand. Her eyes widened, and her lips parted slightly in question. *The lucky coin strikes again.* Even a Randolph had a right to a second chance.

Brice said, "The fire's set. You light it." He found another lantern and left.

Fifteen minutes later, Brice was back with the water. Spring rains had filled the well, and getting the water was easier than giving away beer at a picnic, though finding the bucket in the dark had been another story.

There was a fire blazing in the hearth now. Brice smiled to himself. The familiar hissing and crackling of burning logs and the aroma of warm hickory gave a feeling of comfort and home to the old place. The tension across his back eased for the first time all day.

Firefighter Prudence, on the other hand, wasn't relaxed at all. She stood in front of the hearth, her hair down, kind of wild and untamed, her gaze glued to the flames. She held a shovel in a death grip. A spark popped and had the audacity to fly onto the stone apron of the hearth. Pru swiftly smashed it to smithereens, setting off a terrible *clang* that bounced off the bare walls and jarred Brice to the fillings in his teeth. So much for relaxation!

"Dang, girl."

"What?"

"Put down the shovel. The fireplace is solid stone. We're safe."

She didn't even glance at him. "Can't be sure."

He hadn't seen such determination on someone's face since Johnny Lugers punched out Hank the Hammer for messing with his girl.

Brice set the bucket and lantern on the hearth, then he reached around Pru and pried her fingers free of the shovel. The fresh vanilla scent of her hair filled his lungs and his head. She had incredible hair.

"What are you doing?"

"Preserving my eardrums" is what he said. *Losing my mind over you* is what he thought. She felt small and delicate caged against him for a moment. But he knew she was neither. She was the most determined female he'd ever encountered. Give Pru a job, and it was done if she had to move half of Texas to do it.

He took the shovel as she turned to face him. "This is not Pine Tree Ridge."

Her eyebrows scrunched into a deep *V*.

"I know, I know," he said. "I'm a McCormack—how can you trust me? But this time I have as much at stake as you do. It might be your house, but my new barn's out back, and this is my land. Right?"

Some of the persistence sparking her eyes died. Bone-weary exhaustion took its place. She nodded. He said, "Now I'm going to get those sleeping bags. In the morning we'll have warm water so we can wash up." He hated to say the next words because they would get him into another passel of trouble, but he had to chance it. "There's an outhouse around back. That indoor plumbing I told you about needs help before we can use it."

When she didn't even take a swing at him, he knew she was asleep on her feet. He smiled. Sometimes exhaustion was a good thing. "Sit down, Pru. It's been a tough day." He took off his jacket and spread it out on the floor, before pushing gently on her shoulder, encouraging her to sit. "You okay?"

"Hmm." Her eyes were already half closed as she gazed into the fire, letting the flames hypnotize her into a dreamy state—at least, that's how it worked on him.

"You're sure about the fire?" she asked, her speech slurred a bit.

"It's staying right where it is."

"Promise?"

He smiled. "Cross my heart."

Brice went to get the bags, and when he came back he wasn't surprised to find Pru asleep on the floor, her head cradled in the crook of her arm, her legs bent at the knees. He wasn't even surprised to find the shovel at her side, her arm draped over the handle. Prudence Randolph wasn't the sort of person to make the same mistake twice. Everyone knew that.

He unzipped one sleeping bag and laid it beside her. He slipped off her shoes, and remembered seeing her hot-pink toenails peeking out from under her wedding dress. A smile crept across his lips. He knew he'd never forget Prudence in that dress, without shoes and veil and flowers, looking more lovely than any woman had a right to look.

He ignored the slow, steady thud of his heart, and instead considered how to get Pru into the sleeping bag. If he put one hand on her shoulder and one on her back, he could roll her into the bag and zip her up without even waking her. He owed her that much. It was a good plan—until he touched her shoulder.

Suddenly he was mesmerized by the tendrils of hair framing her face, as firelight wove golds, auburns and reds into spellbinding ribbons of color. Her face held a touch of spring sun, and her lips were smooth, soft and slightly parted. Brice wanted nothing more than to touch them with his own, just as he had only hours ago.

She stirred, her mouth parted just a breath more, and her hair fell to the side, exposing her lovely neck. A hint of vanilla scented the air and every muscle in his body went rock-hard. Desire thrust against the zipper of his jeans, and his blood felt hot in his veins.

Hell, he didn't need this in his life right now. He was tired, completely drained, and didn't have the energy to ward off lust, especially a strong attack like this. All he wanted to do was help Pru into a sleeping bag so that when she woke she wouldn't feel as if someone had tied her body into a pretzel knot. Then he wanted to crawl into his own sleeping bag. He watched the rise and fall of her blouse, of her well-rounded breasts. Actually, he'd rather crawl into Pru's sleeping bag.

He took a deep breath, willing himself to calm down. Yeah, like that was going to work. Gritting his teeth against the hunger building inside him, Brice put his hand on Pru's back and gently rolled her over. Quickly he zipped her tempting body inside. Out of sight, out of mind, he reasoned. Ha!

Brice dropped an armful of logs on the fire, and heat filled the room. He pulled his sleeping bag far away from Pru and the blaze, figuring he was plenty hot enough already. He wanted Pru right now—he wanted her bad—but that was just a biological reaction to a pretty woman. A very pretty woman who happened to be his wife.

But they were enemies, had been since birth. And that would never change, no matter how much Judge Willis—or Brice's screaming hormones—wanted it to.

PRUDENCE'S STOMACH GROWLED with hunger, and she opened her eyes to sunshine streaming through filthy windows. A blob of blue nylon that looked like the cocoon of a really big moth was stretched out on the floor some distance away.

Thin bands of smoke circled from dying embers in the hearth were all that remained of last night's fire. The fire *she* had lit, she reminded herself with satisfaction. The fire Brice had encouraged her to light, she reminded herself again. And he must have zipped her in this sleeping bag as well. She snuggled in a little deeper. Those were nice things for Brice to do, but they couldn't make up for this…this house, as if anyone in their right mind would call this a house.

Looking around, Prudence realized it was in even worse shape than she'd thought. Bigger cracks, more broken windows, crates and boxes here and there, water-stained ceilings. Roof leaks? What a mess.

At the moment, however, she had a more urgent problem. Where had Brice said that outhouse was?

Unzipping her bag, she braced herself for the morning chill that she already felt on her nose and cheeks. On the count of three, she threw off the covers. Yikes! Shivering, she found her shoes, her overnight bag and Brice's jacket on the floor. It fit more like a coat, and that's just what she needed this morning. She made her way to the back door, noticing a mudroom off to one side. To think there was running water but that she couldn't get to it made her insides weep.

She opened the squeaky back door, then closed it

behind her and leaned against it for a moment, letting the sunshine warm her bones. Birds performed an early-morning tweeting serenade as she breathed in the fresh air and noticed the dew that clung to raggedy clumps of grass and scraggly bushes and weeds. The little white run-down house behind a stand of birch trees was probably what she was looking for. All this was incredibly picturesque, real Norman Rockwell stuff, a true slice of rural Americana—and it was something she could very well do without, thank you.

And as outhouses went, she decided as she came out minutes later with the plank door banging shut behind her, this one wasn't just bad. It was horrible! It stunk to high heaven! It had a broken wood seat that actually pinched her, and there wasn't even a Sears Catalog. Wasn't that mandatory in such places?

If Brice tried to convince her to stay in this poor excuse of a house, she'd shoot him, stuff his carcass and hang it over that stone fireplace he liked so much. That way *he* could stay at his precious ranch as long as he wanted, and she could take his truck back to town.

"See you found the facilities," Brice called from the house. The back door stood open, and he was leaning against the paint-chipped frame. His eye looked better—only a bit of purple now with the yellow starting to show more.

Jeans rode low on his hips as he systematically buttoned a clean denim shirt. The tails flapping in the gentle morning breeze gave Pru diminishing glimpses of skin that held a hint of tan. She also caught sight of a fine line of black curly hair bisecting his middle and disappearing into his waistband just below his navel.

She swallowed a whimper as each button closed. By the time Brice secured the last one, her heartbeat had doubled and her insides were mush. How could this happen? She was angry as a cat caught in a thunderstorm because Brice had tricked her into staying in this wretched house. A minute ago she had fantasized about his body being stuffed and mounted. Now all she wanted to do was get her hands on...on his broad shoulders, flat stomach and tight-curled hair that ran down his middle to...to—

"Coffee's on," Brice said. "Should be ready any minute now."

Coffee? Oh yes, she needed it bad. Potfuls of the high-powered stuff to clear her brain and kill her sex drive. Hadn't she read somewhere that caffeine did that? She stole another quick look at Brice, and her stomach somersaulted. Maybe she should get coffee in town, where there were lots and lots of people around to distract her and her hormones.

"We should go, now. This place is—"

"Figured we'd be able to work out our housing problem if we had some food. You've got to be hungry. I sure am."

"Food?" She stopped in her tracks and stared up at him. "You have coffee *and* food?"

"Powdered eggs, some dried meat, juice, some canned chocolate pudding and—"

She pushed past him into the house, catching the aroma of coffee. She could hold on to what was left of her self-control, couldn't she? At least for another half-hour. Brice had food. He had chocolate. Life on a ranch wasn't all bad.

"The coffee's hanging over the fire," he called, following her inside. "I don't have anything cooked yet, but—"

"Give me a pan, then stand aside. My stomach's so empty, it thinks my throat's been cut."

He laughed. It was a great laugh. She hadn't heard it much over the years. Then again, the two of them hadn't had much to laugh together about.

He said, "That doesn't sound like a phrase I've ever heard around the bank. What happened to Prudence Randolph, city-slicker and sophisticated lawyer?"

"She died of starvation a half-hour ago. Which way to the kitchen? You do have a can opener, don't you?"

"Never took you for the cooking kind, Pru."

She arched her left brow and gave him a sassy smile. "I putter in the kitchen once in a while when the cook has the day off. I might have burned down Pine Tree Ridge, but I never burn a casserole."

"Well, hell, Pru, if I'd known that, I'd have taken out more fire insurance and married you a long time ago." Then he snatched her around the waist, twirled her around and kissed her on the cheek. It was a light, friendly kiss, quick and easy, from someone who was having a little fun and appreciated food as much as she did at the moment. It was a little nothing-kiss.

Except, it was Brice's kiss, and that was definitely something.

She didn't want it to be something, of course. She wanted breakfast, or she wanted to skin Brice alive and tap-dance on his entrails for having tricked her. At least, that's what she thought she wanted—until she felt his solid chest touch hers, realized his arm was gently circling her waist, his breath warming her cheek. So she kissed him back, because she was a woman with woman feelings, and she'd simply die if she didn't. Hey, it was his fault. He was the one standing in that blasted doorway looking like the cowboy-of-the-month centerfold, the one who had irresistible kisses, no matter where they were planted.

His breath caught in surprise, and his eyes darkened as he stared at her. She touched his arms, feeling the hard muscles there. He stroked her back. His touch was gentle, caring. No one had hands like Brice, she was sure of it. Her heart thudded, then raced. His tongue grazed against hers, and heat pooled deep in her belly. Her bones turned to rubber. Her brain melted to Silly Putty.

She shouldn't have kissed Brice. It was on impulse, and it was a huge mistake. She should have gone into town for that coffee. She had to stop this now. She was not going to get involved with the guy who made her life miserable. Only, he didn't feel too miserable at all, right now. He felt great, and he made her feel pretty great, too.

She pulled back and stared up at him. "This...is...a really bad idea."

"Yeah." He stepped back from her and stuffed his hands in his back pockets. She was amazed how much she missed his warmth, his touch, his gaze meeting hers.

"We don't want to start anything, Brice. We don't trust or even like each other. Remember me? Prudence Randolph, bounty hunter of all things McCormack? Remember the disagreements we've had over the years? The yelling matches we've had?" She felt as if she was trying to convince herself as much as she was Brice. It was tough doing so while under the influence of strong arms, great hands and dark brown eyes.

"You're right. We're both just tired, not thinking too clearly. And we're hungry, really hungry, and we've been under a lot of stress."

"Yeah, hunger and stress can make people do strange things."

"Glad we got that straightened out."

"Yeah, me too—"

Suddenly steps thundered on the porch, drawing their attention to the front door. There was an angry knock. "Prudence!" called her father. "Are you in there?"

"Brice!" Granddad Wes called.

Pru watched the door fly open and both men stride inside, nearly wedging themselves in the entrance because the idea of one yielding to the other never crossed their minds. She hadn't even heard their cars drive up.

Brice stood beside her, casually draping his arm over her shoulders, then said, "What the hell are you two doing here? Don't either of you believe in knocking?"

Granddad Wes pushed his gray, weather-beaten Stetson to the back of his head and glared at Brice, then Prudence. "I didn't think there was time for knocking, since putting a McCormack and a Randolph together in one spot for any length of time has got to be as much trouble as five rattlers in a canoe. Fact is, I'm surprised as all get-out to see you both alive." He looked from Prudence to Brice and back again. A frown pinched his brow. "Never in all my born days did I figure on seeing a McCormack and a Randolph with their arms around each other, married or not."

"And that's exactly why we're here," Bob Randolph added as he folded his arms across his pristine white dress shirt, giving his daughter a hard look. "To remind you both just who the devil you are, and to end this here marriage once and for all."

Chapter Five

"How'd you find us?" Brice asked.

Granddad Wes stuffed his hands in the pockets of his faded jeans and rocked back on his boot heels. He focused on a spot just beyond Brice's ear. "Well, now, that's a mighty good question—yes, sir, it sure is. As luck would have it, Don Cory was out flying in his Cessna this morning, checking on his herd and all, and spotted your truck parked here. Gave me a call in case I was worried about you. Might friendly thing to do, wouldn't you say? Guess he gave old Randolph here a call, too."

Bob Randolph snarled, "Just who are you calling 'old,' McCormack? You're the prune-face around—"

"That's bull-honkey," Brice said to his granddad. "You can't lie worth diddly, never could. You got Cory to go looking for Pru and me, and Randolph here did the same."

"All I want to know," Bob Randolph said, squaring his shoulders in defense, "is why in thunder Pru would marry a McCormack in the first place? Makes no sense at all."

Wes said to Brice, "Don't you see that it's all wrong for you to be married to...her?" He nodded at Pru.

"For once in seventy years," chimed in Bob Randolph, "a McCormack's right. This marriage needs to end right now. Today."

Brice sighed and exchanged a look with Pru. They both knew that was impossible, unless every McCormack and Randolph felt like doing jail time whenever they tangled. Serenity would lose a big chunk of its population to the county jail if Judge Willis carried out his threat. And Willis wasn't known for idle threats.

Brice said, "I've got news for you both—Pru and I are exactly where we want to be at this very moment."

Granddad Wes said, "Then you're making a big mistake, boy. We need you back at the main house, to run the ranch."

"With you, Derek, Aunt Rose and Mamma there, it's crowded enough at the house, don't you think?"

"You're the one everybody relies on to make decisions and keep things going. You always have been."

"I'm a five-minute ride away, for crying out loud."

"Can't you see that this marriage idea is the Randolphs' way of getting their conniving clutches into the Half-Circle?"

"Ha!" countered Bob Randolph. "It's the McCormacks who promise the earth to get what they want, then leave you hanging high and dry." He turned to Prudence. "Look where this McCormack's got you living, girl. A miserable shack. This place is a dump, and I'm not having any daughter of mine living in a McCormack dump." He huffed and turned the color of a red spring poppy. "I ask you, is this any way to treat a wife? A loved one? I should say not. Brice is after something. Look at what McCormacks did to your great-granddaddy, and Brice here's one of them. Fact is, he's head of 'em. Keep it in mind."

Prudence glanced up at Brice. He felt her stiffen, obviously remembering how he'd stretched the truth to the breaking point to get her here, where he wanted her.

Bob said, "I can tell by that look on your face, Prudence, that Brice has done something else besides move you to this hovel that's making you wonder just what his motives really are."

Brice bristled. "Like hell. I gave your daughter this house. It's a fine house. It needs work, but we can fix it—"

"You what?" Wes's eyes bulged and the purple vein at his left temple throbbed. "You gave away part of the Half-Circle to a Randolph? Have you gone plumb loco?"

Brice's throat went as dry as a pond in a Texas summer; suddenly he was feeling uneasy about what he'd done. "I only gave her the house, not the land." The excuse sounded lame even to his ears.

Granddad Wes gulped air, looking like a landed fish. "That means I'm standing smack-dab in the middle of a...a Randolph house? Have mercy! I've never been inside a Randolph house." He wiped his brow with the back of his hand, clearly stricken. "What did I tell you? Prudence here's already gotten her way, poisoning you against your own and leading you down the garden path so you'd give her the Half-Circle. How could you go and do that?" His eyes narrowed to thin slits. "Has this Randolph woman gone and bewitched you, boy?"

Pru slipped from Brice's arm and planted her fists on her hips. She glared at Wes. "I didn't poison anyone about anything, and I do not bewitch."

Pru might be outraged at Granddad Wes's accusation, but Wes was right, Brice realized. The Half-Circle was the life of the McCormack family. Even if the house was newly acquired and dilapidated, it was still part of the ranch. Brice should never have given it away, even if it was only for the time he was married to Pru. What had he been thinking? What if there was some glitch and he couldn't get it back? What if Pru refused to divorce him unless he gave her the house *and* the land? He wasn't bewitched. He was a plain old idiot.

But instead of saying that, Brice continued. "It's just a house, Granddad. Someplace for Pru and me to live." Pru smiled up at him way too sweetly, as daggers shot from her eyes. Today was going no better than yesterday; in fact, it was worse. He'd lost part of his ranch, and he and Pru were more at odds than ever. How could they straighten out this feud if the two of them couldn't even get along? "I'm still around to run the ranch and see to the oil wells. As far as you and the family are concerned, that's what's important. Pru and I will take care of the rest. We know what we're doing." He nearly choked on his own words.

"Well," Granddad Wes said, "don't go expecting me or any of your kin to come visiting in a Randolph house. It's the last place on earth we're aiming to be."

Bob Randolph said, "And I sure don't cotton to being on McCormack land any more than I have to, even if Randolphs do have a rightful claim to it now."

Granddad Wes rounded on Bob Randolph. "That's nothing but hogwash. You and your kin got no claim at all on anything McCormack."

"Says who?" Bob Randolph and Granddad Wes met toes and noses.

"Says me. You're nothing but a liar and a cheat and—"

"Stop," Pru said, glaring at her father. "This is getting us nowhere. Brice and I are married. Your fighting with Wes is not going to change that." Her voice was laced with steel. In all the years Brice had known her, he'd never heard her use that tone with her father. "Dad, you...you have to go."

Bob Randolph's eyes widened to cover half his face. "I beg your pardon?"

For a second Brice watched Pru decide between fight or flight. Fighting her dad was not typical of Pru—Brice felt certain of that. He watched as she straightened her shoulders, then walked to her dad, firmly took him by the elbow and led him out the door. Maybe today wasn't such a bad day, after all.

Bob Randolph looked completely thunderstruck, as Pru said, "I'll see you in town tomorrow, Dad. I'll be at the bank bright and early." She kissed him on the cheek and propelled him toward his Lincoln.

Brice put his hand on Granddad Wes's shoulders and escorted him out. "I'll check on that new stock we have coming in this afternoon. We can talk then. But you have to keep in mind, I'm staying married to Pru." Brice opened the door to Granddad Wes's pickup, and the older man got in.

With Pru at his side, Brice watched the Lincoln bounce down the lane, looking as if a pogo stick were attached to the undercarriage. The red truck didn't fare much better. He and Pru waved, smiled and looked lovey-dovey—until the two vehicles turned the last bend.

Then Pru faced him. Her eyebrows narrowed, and her back went ramrod straight. She glared, and her pupils were tiny little dots. "You did just what my dad said, you conned me. Told me a pack of lies to get me out here where you wanted me." She pulled in a deep breath. "You did just what your granddaddy did, and I fell for it."

"Pru! I gave you a house, for crying out loud. A piece of the Half-Circle."

"Big whoop. You can have your doggone house back if you just take me into town. We'll live there."

He tramped toward his truck, fully intending to do as asked. After all, then he would get his house back. He really liked this house, and he'd fix it up with or without Pru. But he suddenly stopped, then retraced his steps back to where Pru was standing. "Going into town is going to create more problems than it's going to solve."

Her eyes widened. "Because you don't happen to like town? Because it's not your wonderful ranch? Because you'll have to drive—"

"Because, city girl, town's neutral territory."

"What's that supposed to mean?"

He pulled in a deep breath. "You think I conned you to get you out here—well, maybe I did. You got a piece of the Half-Circle, and I'm not feeling too good about that, either. So, we're both mad. But we have to stay right here until this marriage ends one way or the other."

"In your dreams, Brice McCormack."

Her eyes flashed like blue lightning, and a gentle breeze tangled her hair that was down and mussed instead of pinned up as usual. Did she have to look so damn beautiful when they were both spitting mad?

"Pru, think about it. If we live anywhere else, we'll have to put in a revolving door because neither family will stop trying to convince each of us to leave the other. There'll be fights and arguments and arrests galore. We'll spend most of our time in front of Judge Willis, bailing our families out of trouble because they're fighting over us. I'll never get any ranching done, and you can kiss tax deadlines goodbye. No one will ever believe we're happily married, and Willis will be madder than a beaver with a toothache.''

He ran his fingers through his hair, then continued. ''If we stay here, neither family will bother us. You heard them.'' Brice nodded toward the retreating clouds of dust. ''McCormacks won't step in a Randolph home, and Randolphs won't step on McCormack land, making this a perfect place to hide out till Willis figures out he made a mistake marrying us.''

''But...but the house is a dump.''

He gave her a hard look. ''I said I can fix it, and I can.''

''When? In between roping and branding and whatever else you do?''

''It's this house or Randolph-McCormack bedlam. Take your pick. I'm going inside to cook us something to eat.'' He turned toward the house and called over his shoulder, ''Let me know what you decide.''

He expected to hear some sort of affirmative response to his proposal. After all, what other choice did they have? Instead, he heard his pickup roar to life. He turned in time to see it tear down the lane, spewing gravel and dirt, and hopping in and out of every pothole in sight. Well, hell, when he told her to get a four-wheel drive, he sure as hell didn't mean take his.

Damn the woman! Brice kicked at a clod of dirt, sending it airborne till it smacked against a tree. He had no idea if Pru was coming back, staying in town, or if she was going to keep on driving right out of Serenity and put this whole ordeal behind her.

The only thing Brice did know was that if he intended to meet up with Granddad Wes, he had a mighty long walk back to the main house. He also knew Granddad and the rest of his kin would give him no end of grief once they learned just why Brice was on foot.

Being married to Prudence Randolph was a real pain in the backside, and he intended to tell her precisely that, *if* he ever laid eyes on her and his truck again.

PRUDENCE TURNED OFF the lane—or as Brice called it, the two-track—and headed toward town. She needed to think things out and wanted nothing more than to drive straight to her house—her real house—and get a shower, clean clothes, hot food and chocolate. She always thought better with something chocolate in her stomach.

But she couldn't do any of those things. In fact, she couldn't go anywhere looking as she did in day-old clothes that she'd slept in. She caught a glimpse of her reflection in the rearview mirror and bit back a scream. Puffy eyes, wild hair, no makeup. The day after her wedding people would ask questions. And she'd be sorely tempted to tell them what was going on, and that Brice McCormack was a no-account, double-crossing con artist who had given her a house that should be burned to the ground.

Of course, then everyone would know their marriage was a sham. The feud would be worse, Willis would know it was her fault, and Randolphs and McCormacks would go to jail. Not that she gave a gnat's eye about the McCormacks going to jail.

There was one person, however, who already knew all the sordid details, wouldn't mind listening to a few more, and would feed her if she dropped enough hints—Sunny Willis. Taking the next left, Prudence headed for the Willis house. With all her might she hoped that Sunny was home and that the judge wasn't. Prudence was in no mood to see that man, since he'd gotten her into this mess.

Prudence parked Brice's truck outside the Willises' sprawling ranch, followed the sidewalk lined with daffodils, then rang the bell. As she waited, Prudence gazed across the sprawling front lawn. It was hard to believe that just yesterday there'd been white tents, guests, a marriage ceremony and fistfights here. A truly memorable wedding in anyone's book.

When she didn't get an answer on the second bong of the bell, Prudence followed the brick walkway around to the back to check Sunny's gardens. Sure enough, she found Sunny elbow-deep in peat moss. Her hair was not the perfectly coiffured style of yesterday, but was loose and springy, and she was singing a sweet lullaby to beds of pansies and tulips.

"Well, bless my soul," she said, when Pru caught her eye. "It's the newlyweds."

"Make that *newlywed*," Pru corrected. "Brice is back at the Half-Circle playing with his cows. Today I think it's Follow the Leader." She stroked her chin. "Actually, right about now he's probably *walking* to the Half-Circle."

Sunny raised one eyebrow. "Walking? From where?"

Prudence shrugged. "From the old Dillard place. I sort of borrowed his truck."

Sunny let loose a carefree giggle, then wiped her arms and hands on a towel. "Sounds interesting. Let's go on inside and have some tea, and you can tell me about it."

"Any chance of having a side order of eggs, bacon and toast with that?" So much for hinting.

Sunny smiled. "Brice isn't feeding you? No wonder you snatched his truck out from under him." She turned toward the back door of the ranch, and Prudence fell into step beside her as the woman continued. "Since you're wearing the same clothes you had on when you left here to bail out your kin yesterday, I take it your wedding night was a mite...rocky?"

"As the Grand Canyon."

Sunny reached for the doorknob, then paused and faced Prudence. "Fiddlesticks. I saw how he kissed you and how you kissed him right back, after the judge pronounced you husband and wife."

Prudence felt her stomach flip at the thought. It

did a double flip when she thought of Brice kissing her this morning.

Sunny grinned. "From the look on your face right now, I'd say your wedding night was more Appalachian Mountains than Grand Canyon." They entered the kitchen, and after washing her hands, Sunny took eggs and bacon from the fridge. "You can build roads through the Appalachians, you know. I'll cook—you sit down and think about road building."

Prudence parked herself in a ladder-back chair and propped her elbow on the oak table, resting her chin in her palm. She watched Sunny start up the bacon, then crack eggs. The heavenly aroma of an old-fashioned, artery-clogging breakfast soon filled the room. It was a great room, the perfect kitchen. She'd die for a kitchen like this.

"Brice and I don't want to build roads. All we want is for your husband to realize he's made a big mistake getting us married—the feud's worse now than ever. Then we can all go back to the way things were before he got his lame-brained idea."

Sunny turned the bacon, then put bread in the toaster. "Well, dear, you're going to have a mighty long wait. Admitting he's wrong isn't one of the judge's strong suits. Maybe you and Brice should concentrate on ending the feud, instead."

Prudence felt her head swim. "That's never going to happen. We'd have to undo seventy years of bickering. It's impossible."

"The longest journey starts with one step, and that step was getting a McCormack and Randolph hitched. Think about it. All you have to do now is get the McCormacks and Randolphs to agree on just one little thing at a time. Then pretty soon they'll be agreeing on everything. The feud will end faster that way than waiting for the judge to change that stubborn mind of his."

Sunny slid the eggs from the skillet onto a plate, snatched the toast and added the bacon. She placed the food on the table.

Prudence dug into the eggs, swallowed a mouthful, forced herself to slow down so she wouldn't gulp everything, then said, "But what kind of stuff would a McCormack and Randolph ever agree on? When the sun comes up? When it sets? That's about all they'd ever see eye-to-eye on."

Sunny poured two cups of tea, set out a plate of sugar cookies. She claimed a chair on the other side of the big oak table. "Seems to me some sort of cause might work. Give people a common goal and bingo—" Sunny snapped her fingers "—Randolphs and McCormacks will come together faster than two gossips on a summer night. Finding the right cause is the trick. No one's come up with that yet. I started the garden club for that very reason, and didn't have much luck at all. Do you know the Randolphs and McCormacks spent two whole meetings arguing over the color of yellow daffodils?"

"Sounds like you want to see this feud end every bit as much as I do." Prudence bit into the best toast she'd ever eaten.

"Oh, my stars, yes." Sunny's eyes sparkled.

"When the judge retires, he's promised me a trip to England. I hear tell the gardens there are plumb delightful. For the past five years the judge has said we're going, and for the past five years this ongoing rhubarb's gotten worse and worse. The judge is afraid to leave, afraid what will happen to Serenity while he's gone. If this feud doesn't end soon, the judge and I will be too decrepit to go anywhere except an old folks home."

"I don't think you or the judge will ever be decrepit. Maybe if *you* tell him the marriage has done more harm than good it would help. Tell him that just this morning Dad and Granddad Wes showed up at the house, and Brice and I nearly had World War Three in the living room."

Sunny's eyes widened. "We? You and Brice—a Randolph and a McCormack—have a house? Where you live *together?*" A little smile tugged at Sunny's lips as she absently selected a sugar cookie. She nibbled the edges. "Hmm, imagine that. You have a house."

"It's not exactly a house, Sunny. More like a hovel. It's the old Dillard place, remember?" Prudence eyed the cookies, wondering if Sunny had any chocolate-chip ones stashed somewhere. "Brice deeded it to me for as long as we're married. It was a rotten trick to get me out to the Half-Circle."

Sunny arched her eyebrows. "*Your* house, you say? On the Half-Circle. My, my, my. This gets better all the time." Sunny drummed her fingers on the pine tabletop. "You own the house, Brice owns the land. Can't remember a McCormack and Randolph ever being this chummy before."

"We're not 'chummy.'" *Most of the time we're not chummy,* her conscience amended. "We don't even trust each other. Don't even like each other." Usually.

As if she hadn't heard a word, Sunny stared off into space, muttering, "This is mighty unusual, mighty unusual, indeed." Her fingers continued their drumming.

Suddenly, she hopped up and smacked the tabletop with the flat of her hand, making Prudence jump in her seat. "Time's a wastin', girl. We've got to build on this. There's work to be done."

"Huh? Build on what—?"

Sunny snatched cups and plates off the table in one swift movement and took them to the sink.

"But...but my breakfast?" Prudence watched her food go into the garbage disposal. Was life ever fair?

"English gardens are at their perkiest in June, so that doesn't give us much time to set things to rights in Serenity."

"There's always next year, Sunny. Or even the year after that. English gardens have been around for a really long time."

"Horsefeathers, I want to go this year. We gotta get a move on."

"But the feud's been going on for seventy years, how can we—"

"First off," Sunny interrupted, ignoring all protests, "you've got to fix up that house of yours so both families think this marriage is going to last till you and Brice drop dead. Everyone will see that McCormacks and Randolphs *can* work together. It's a mighty good place to start."

Pru wagged her head. "Brice and I can't do anything together. How are we going to fix up a house? We fight, like...McCormacks and Randolphs."

"Just pretend to get along." Sunny narrowed her eyes and stared at Prudence. "You want this feud to end, too, don't you? Make the Dillard place a kind of monument to peace and goodwill. Like the U.N. Then think of some way to get the rest of your kin together. Like...like a barn raising."

"Sunny, Randolphs don't build barns. A little porch furniture now and then, but no barns."

"Well, you and Brice are sure to come up with something. Now, go on down the hall and wash up quick-like. Borrow one of my sweaters if you want. We've got to get that house in working order—and the sooner the better."

Pru watched the cookies being dumped back into a ceramic jar that looked like a giant sunflower. She didn't even get one cookie crumb. "Sunny, listen to me. You're not getting the whole picture, here. The Dillard place has no heat, no running water, no phone. There's stuff piled in boxes. The roof leaks, for heaven's sake." Prudence spread her hands wide. "It's utterly hopeless."

Sunny looked her right in the eye. "Nothing in this whole wide world is hopeless, dear. Not ending this here feud and certainly not ending my expectations of getting to England this year. My brother Ralph is a plumber. He can get your hot water and other plumbing needs going lickety-split. The hardware store always has names of people who can check out the furnace, and one phone call should get the electricity working. The judge has friends all over town who can help us out. You'll see—once you have the comforts of home, the rest will fall into place.'' Her eyes were as bright as sun reflecting off a lake. ''But do it quick. I've got to make plane reservations. Mercy, we'll have to get passports. And new luggage. I like the suitcases with those little wheels on the bottom. And cameras and film, lots of film.''

Prudence headed for the bathroom to make herself presentable. Coming here had been a huge mistake. She should have stayed back at the ranch, eaten powdered eggs and argued with Brice, because now things were worse than before. She couldn't just wait around till the judge came to his senses and let her and Brice out of the damnable marriage. She and Brice were going to have to come up with some way to end the feud themselves, or Sunny and the judge would never make it to England.

Of course, that wasn't the only reason. If Sunny was right, the judge would never admit the marriage was a bad idea, and she and Brice could be trapped together for a really long time.

That was one thing she didn't want to happen. The constant fighting would be awful. And there was the problem of Brice, the man. She sure couldn't resist

Brice on a physical level for a really long time. The kiss this morning proved that. But she also couldn't get involved with a man who tricked her, and whom she didn't trust and who owed his allegiance to his family. The feud had to end—that was the only solution.

Maybe this house idea would work out. Brice wanted to stay there, thought it was the best idea since the wheel. Like Sunny said, it would create the impression that she and Brice were a happily married couple, and the Randolphs and McCormacks could work together in harmony. It was a start. She and Brice could build on it. Spread the word that this marriage was the best thing ever. Maybe more Randolphs and McCormacks would start talking and getting together, like the judge said. It was worth a try.

BRICE SWIPED his Resistol from his head and ran his shirt sleeve over his dust-smeared face. Humidity hung heavy in the air as a bank of clouds collected on the horizon. Bringing in new stock was always hard work. They had to be fed and watered, and they were skittish as hell, especially with a storm heading this way.

Derek slapped Brice on the back. "Some fine-looking cows there. You always did know how to pick 'em."

"They'll do. We can run 'em over to the Dillard place tomorrow. No sense in moving them in nasty weather."

"Speaking of the Dillard place—" Derek arched

his brows "—how is Prudence Randolph McCormack this morning?" Derek nudged Brice in a man-to-man way.

"Okay." Brice walked faster, and Derek kept pace. All day Brice had gotten the third-degree about Pru. He'd kept his responses to one-syllable words or grunts. He was tired of questions, and he was damn tired of grunting.

"Heard you walked on over here this morning," Derek continued. "Trouble in paradise?"

"Nope." Brice opened the door to Derek's four-by-four, as Derek asked, "Going somewhere?"

"Yep." He brought the truck to life, then took off down the road, with Derek yelling that this was his truck, and something about Brice being of questionable parentage for taking it.

Too bad. Derek would get his truck back when Brice got *his* back. Besides, Derek could borrow Mamma's truck or one of the cousins' vehicles if he had the need. How could Pru have left Brice stranded? How could she not tell him where she was going? How could she have the softest lips, silkiest hair and sexiest little body, and be conniving enough to fast-shuffle him out of the Dillard house?

Clouds cut the sunlight in half and thunder echoed in the distant hills as he pulled Derek's pickup next to his own. Well, well. The troublemaker was back.

Brice stomped up what was left of the front steps of the house and yanked open the door. "Prudence!" They needed to talk, right now. "Pru?" He searched the living room, kitchen, mudroom and storage room.

They needed to set some ground rules. "Prudence?" He went upstairs. He and Pru needed to get a few things straight if they were going to live together, like where in blue blazes that would be.

He searched the front bedroom, then went into the back one. And Pru needed to know his truck was *his* truck, and that if she wanted one, she could buy one of her very—

Brice stopped dead at a thumping noise at the window. He went there and looked outside as a leather shoe hit the glass with a loud *thawmp,* making him jump back. "What the—?"

Peering outside again, Brice saw two khaki-covered legs dangling from the roof. One foot was bare, one had on a familiar leather shoe, and both looked as if they were scrambling to get a toehold on a ladder—except there wasn't a ladder in sight.

Chapter Six

Brice's heart stopped. Panic gripped his chest. He threw open the window and got a bare foot in the nose, knocking his hat clean off his head. "Prudence, is that you?"

"Brice!"

The legs flailed again, and Brice stepped back.

"Get me down!"

"I can't get you from in here. I can't reach you. The overhang's too far out. What the hell are you doing up there?"

"Falling?"

"Hold on. I'm coming." Brice tore for the steps, the clatter of his boots on wood echoing through the dark rooms. He ran out the back door, then looked up and called, "Where's the ladder?" He figured she was about fifteen feet off the ground.

"In front. I—" Pru's words died in her throat as the gutter she was holding on to began to pull away from the roof with a sickening *creak.* "Brice!" Her legs gyrated as she kicked the air.

"Hold still! You'll make things worse."

She looked down at him for a split second, her matter-of-fact lawyer face well in place. "Things could be worse?" The gutter gave way another inch, and her eyes widened.

"There's no time to get the ladder. I'll catch you."

"Yeah, right. Get the ladder."

"What the hell is that supposed to mean?"

"You think I stole your truck and house. You're a McCormack. Want me to go on here?"

"Pru, you can trust me." The gutter pulled again, this time loosening the entire section attached to the roof. He held out his arms. "It won't hold much longer!"

"But—"

"Drop, dammit! Now! You've got to trust me, Pru."

She looked up at the gutter, down to Brice, back to the gutter. Then she let go, falling neatly into his arms and sending them both tumbling backward onto the ground, and down a hill. She was on top of him, he on top of her, she back on him. They rolled over the grass, rocks and sticks, then up against a tree, his back smacking against the trunk, knocking the wind right out of him.

They lay there for a second, him sandwiched between the tree and Pru, gasping for air, before he heard her say, "Damn!"

Pru never said "damn." Since her face was pressed to his shoulder, he felt her breath coming in quick pants. "You okay?"

"Lost my other shoe. They were Italian."

Brice exhaled a lungful of air in one long swoosh of relief. "Yeah, ain't life a bitch. You all right or not?"

When she didn't answer for a few moments, he tucked his finger under her chin and tipped her face to his. Her eyes were blue-black, covering half her face. She bit her bottom lip, and he felt her tremble. One lonely tear trickled down her left cheek.

Dear lord! He hadn't been ready for that tear. If she'd yelled at the gutter, called it disreputable names or maybe thrown a rock at the house, or even him for getting her out here in the first place—*that* he'd have been ready for. But not the tear.

Pru was terrified, and he realized with a start that he absolutely hated the thought of her being terrified about anything. All her smart-ass cracks and jokes were for show—just bluster. Another one of those Randolph-facing-a-McCormack episodes. He never imagined Pru was so good at covering up what she really felt.

Not that she was the only one who did that sort of thing. Underneath all his joking, he'd been scared half to death, too. He could have dropped her. She could have been seriously hurt. What if he hadn't been here at all? Then he could have lost Pru…forever.

His stomach rolled as that unexpected thought embedded itself in his brain. A slice of cold-blooded fear shot clear through him. Until this very minute, he hadn't appreciated how much he never wanted to be without Pru in his life.

Thunder rumbled long and deep overhead. It shook the earth beneath them, charged the atmosphere and whipped gentle breezes into gusting winds. Right now, he didn't give two hoots in Hades what Pru's last name was, or his, either. The feud that was older than him and Pru put together didn't matter a lick. The only thing he cared about this minute was Pru, that she was safe and in his arms, so he kissed her...because he needed to reaffirm the fact that she was okay more than he needed to breathe.

Pru pulled in a quick breath of surprise, her eyes turning blue as the star-studded sky at midnight on the wide open plain. She tasted warm, sweet and giving, and when he took his lips from hers, her mouth remain parted, inviting his return. Desire coursed hot in his veins. His fingers shook, as much from the fear of losing her as the realization of what was happening between them. He brushed her hair from her forehead and kissed her there. His heart raced. Passion tensed every muscle, and when she wound her arms around his neck and kissed him back, he thought he'd died and gone straight to heaven.

He switched off the voice inside his head that screamed this was a less than brilliant thing to do and ran his fingers through her incredible hair. For a second he pulled back, watching her lush auburn curls framing her beautiful face. She looked like a goddess or a classic painting by an old master. He didn't say a word and neither did Pru, both knowing that words too often spoiled everything.

Her breath quickened, he could feel the rapid rise

and fall of her chest. His head reeled. His soul soared. He felt truly connected to someone for the first time in his life. He kissed her again, feeling his desire for her build faster than he imagined possible. A crack of lightning split the sky, and warm rain fell. Pru brought her lips to his again, and he knew in his heart that they'd belonged together like this for a very long time. But no matter how wonderful her kisses were, getting intimately involved with Pru would end in certain disaster. Just look at what happened to Romeo and Juliet. Good grief!

Using every ounce of self-control he possessed, he took his lips from hers. "We can't do this, Pru. We'll add more problems to the ones we already have." Lightning crackled around them. "We have to get out of this storm now."

PRU SAT on the stone hearth, thankful to be in dry clothes and out of the rain. At least, that's what she tried to tell herself, instead of wishing she was still outside kissing Brice. 'Course she could be kissing him inside, too, except that he was puttering in the kitchen.

She watched the crackling fire and listened to the rain pound the roof and slap the windows. An occasional rumble of thunder rattled the panes, momentarily drowning out the plink-plinging of water dripping into pans, buckets and every other container she and Brice could find in the old boxes stacked along the wall.

Deep down inside Pru wondered if this miserable

house would hold together long enough to get repaired the way Sunny had suggested. Not so deep down inside, Pru wondered if her temporary insanity was curable, because she must have been insane to kiss Brice McCormack the way she did. What had she been thinking?

She hadn't been thinking. That was the whole trouble. Now she was in deep doodoo because kissing Brice had been…really nice. Her conscience pricked. All right, all right, it was terrific, wonderful, stupendous. The angels sang, the sun dimmed. Happy? That might ease her conscience, but it sure didn't ease her hormones. Not that it really mattered, because she and Brice could never take this kissing thing any further, no matter how great he was at it.

He might have caught her when she needed catching, but that didn't mean she could trust him on all fronts, and she wasn't about to get emotionally involved with someone she couldn't trust. He'd tricked her once since they were married, and there was no reason to believe he wouldn't do it again if it benefited his family.

Family was his main priority in life, just as it was hers, and that wasn't likely to change for either of them, no matter how great they kissed.

"Soup's on," Brice said as he came into the room. "At least, it will be as soon as I hang this pot over the fire. Are you getting warm?"

Warm? After what had happened outside less than an hour ago she'd probably be warm as toast for the rest of her life. "We've got to talk, Brice."

He heaved a huge sigh as he ran his hand around the back of his neck. ''You're right. I thought we'd get into something dry and eat first, then—'' he shrugged ''—we can move into town.''

''What?''

''Town. Where we won't be so...together like this. We can't get involved, Pru. You know that as well as I do. You're not willing to give up being a Randolph, and I'm always going to be a McCormack, which means a real relationship between us is out. We'll never agree on anything, and would probably sell each other down the river if it would benefit our families. Right?''

''Blast it, Brice, now is not the time to come up with this brilliant idea of moving to town and not being together. Just this morning you said the ranch was a great place to live and we should stay here. Any of this sound familiar?''

''That was before you and I scorched the ground outside less than an hour ago. We'll move to town, into one of those cracker boxes you like so well. It won't be neutral territory like this ranch is, so our families will drive us nuts and try to split us up. There will be lots of fights, and Willis will have to realize he made a big mistake.''

The lights suddenly came on, brightening the room. Brice's eyes widened. ''We have...electricity? How'd that happen?''

''The electric fairy. He paid us a visit while you were off doing cow stuff. His efforts just got knocked out for a while because of the storm. We also have a new hot-water heater, and kitchen appliances are coming tomorrow."

"You did all that? In one day?"

"Furniture's been ordered, the plumber's scheduled to plumb, and a new roof is on the books for the end of the week. Since you weren't around, I even risked life and limb to put a tarp over the old roof, 'cause that's what the roofer said to do so that the workmen coming in the morning—"

"Workmen?"

"Actually, it's work*people* because three are men and three are women. The Ross family. They run Restorations by Ross, and said they could rehab this house. All day, and I do mean all day, I've lied my heart out convincing everyone in town who would listen that we—as in you and me—are in hog heaven, making a home, working together as husband and wife, showing the whole wide Serenity world that McCormacks and Randolphs can get along. Sunny Willis said fixing this place up would be a good first step in ending the feud, because her dear husband is not now or ever about to give up on his idea of us being married."

"How'd Sunny Willis get into this?"

"She wants to go to England this year."

"England?"

"It's a garden thing."

Brice pinched the bridge of his nose and shook his head.

"Bottom line is we're stuck out here," she said,

"and we're stuck with each other till there's some kind of peace between our dear families."

Brice paced the floor in front to the hearth, then looked back to her. "Okay, we can do this. We'll just steer clear of each other, that's all. I work, you work—that eats up a lot of the day. You sleep upstairs, I sleep downstairs. We'll never see each other. Right?"

"Right. How hard can it be for a Randolph and a McCormack to stay away from each other?"

IT WAS REALLY, really hard for her and Brice to stay away from each other, Prudence realized when she got home from work the next day. Not only did she miss him to the point of getting very little done on the tax forms that needed to be turned in by week's end, but also there were ten messages on the answering machine from people wanting Brice right now and obviously expecting her, the new devoted wife, to know where her husband was.

One of the McCormack's oil rigs was down, and Brice was needed to make some oilman-type decision. But no one knew where to find Mr. Brice McCormack.

Her first thought was to call the Half-Circle and see if Brice was there, but she felt certain the oil people had already done that. Besides, she'd run naked through town before she'd call the McCormack house. Didn't Brice have a cell phone or pager or something so people could get hold of him all the time?

She kicked off her high heels and undid the top button of the new suit jacket that she'd worn to work. As she looked out the front window of the ranch house, she took the pins from her hair, letting it tumble to her shoulders, feeling more relaxed than she had all day.

Late-afternoon sun skimmed over the new-green treetops and cast a silvery glow across the weed-filled yard. Where in blue blazes was that man? How was she going to explain to all these callers that she didn't have the foggiest idea where her new husband was?

If she said he was in town and it turned out he was doing cow business, she'd feel as if she'd failed New Wife 101, and the gossips might start spreading the rumor that all wasn't as it seemed at the Randolph-McCormack house. That wouldn't help end the feud—it would be like adding a squirt of gasoline to it.

And why wasn't Brice around so she could at least see him when she came home from work? Maybe talk to him? Maybe touch his hand? After that, they could stay away from each other.

Suddenly a cow, then two cows, then more came into view down by the new barn. A low, mellow mooing filled the air. It was kind of charming in a ranchy sort of way. She almost expected to see John Wayne moseying across the yard, calling, ''Howdy, pilgrim.'' Instead, she saw a man on horseback herding the cattle into a pen.

At first she thought it was Brice, who was even

better than John Wayne, but looking again she realized it was Derek. He would know where Brice was. She would just have to watch what she said so she didn't look too ignorant of her husband's whereabouts. Men gossiped as much as women ever did. If you wanted to get something around town fast, just tell the guys.

After slipping her shoes back on, she left the house and tiptoed across the mushy ground, heading for the barn. The sun warmed her head and back, and a sky as clear as an expensive diamond stretched out in all directions to meet the rolling green hills. It sure wasn't town. When she looked out the window of Randolph House, she saw the Randolph garage or her uncle Roy's house next door, or Grandma Eulah's house across the street surrounded with yellow roses.

Derek noticed her coming toward him, and he headed her way. The pounding of hoofs made the ground under her feet vibrate, and the smells of horse, good leather, and a hardworking man filled her head as he pulled up his horse next to her. Till now, she hadn't realized just how intoxicating those smells could be. "Hi, new sister-in-law."

Smiling, Derek tipped his hat to her the way cowboys have been doing forever. He nodded toward the house. "Hear you and Brice are fixing the Dillard place up right special. It's the talk of the town. No one can believe a McCormack and a Randolph are actually working together." Derek pushed his dusty gray hat farther back on his head. "So, when are you having me over for dinner?"

Prudence stared up at Derek. She hadn't expected his friendliness, and never would she have expected him to want to be a dinner guest. He was a McCormack, after all. "You'd come?"

"With bells on. I couldn't pass up an offer for free food, and I'd like to get to know the gal who put a burr under my brother's saddle and got him hitched. Never seen anyone get to him the way you do. 'Course, I'm still wondering what got you and Brice together in the first place. Beats the heck out of me and everybody else in this town."

"You wouldn't believe me if I told you." Before Derek had a chance to ask what she was talking about, she added, "Brice is with you, isn't he." She made it sound as if it could be a statement or a question, so she wouldn't seem too clueless.

"We brought the cattle over together." Derek pointed beyond the barn. "But we had to take a longer route because of the hard rain last night. Brice is helping out a cow and calf that got themselves into a pickle. He'll be here in a bit. Miss him?"

"Oh, yeah. Sure. A lot. Yessirree Bob."

Derek gave her a questioning look, as if she'd lost her mind. She guessed she was overdoing the caring wife routine. "There's a problem at one of the oil rigs. They need your brother's input ASAP."

"Well, doggies! I've been telling him to get one of those satellite phones for when he's on the range. But does he listen to me? Heck, no. When he's with his cattle he figures everything else will just have to sit and wait its turn. I'd go fetch him, but I've got to mind the herd, get them settled down for the night with feed and water. You can go get him, though. Just take the truck over the next two ridges and follow the path.''

Terrific. What was she going to say now? *No, I don't really care an ant's ear about oil wells?* That didn't sound very wifey. ''Great idea.''

''Keep the truck on top of the hills and avoid the gullies where there's still water. You'll be fine. Follow the way the herd came, you'll see the trampled grass. It'll take you right to Brice.'' Derek eyed her clothes. ''Nice duds. Don't be getting out of the truck. It's real muddy out there, after the rain last night.''

''Believe me, I wouldn't think of it.'' Prudence picked her way over clumps of mud and made it to Brice's truck. For a second she looked back at the house, realizing the workmen—workpeople—had covered the roof. They had erected scaffolding, too. It looked a lot stronger than the house, but at least the place had the appearance of a Randolph-McCormack home-in-progress. That was the whole point.

Before she got in the truck, she straightened the blanket she'd thrown over the seat to protect her suit that morning when she took the truck in to work. A cowboy's truck wasn't the most fitting place for designer clothes, but her Lincoln would never make it here. She climbed in the truck, smoothed out her linen skirt so it wouldn't wrinkle, started the engine. She headed for the path beyond the barn.

For ten minutes she followed the cow trail. The truck lumbered over the rolling fields, and she avoided the low areas, as Derek had advised. As country went, this was pretty enough. The warming spring earth had a special rich smell that she'd never known about. The air out here felt cleaner, and the sun seemed to shine a bit brighter. The sky was brilliant.

Finally, up ahead, Prudence saw a swollen pond and a black horse hitched to a tree limb. As she got closer, Brice came into view. He was pulling on a rope tied around a cow who was obviously stuck stomach-deep in mud. The cow mooed sorrowfully. Being careful not to end up in the same predicament as the cow, Prudence gave the pond filled to overflowing with spring rain a wide berth, and stopped not too far from Brice. She leaned out the window and called his name.

He did a quick look, then a double take. "Pru?"

Funny how she was getting used to that name, at least from Brice. If he called her anything else, she probably wouldn't know he was talking to her. 'Course, if anyone else dared to call her Pru…well, they'd better run for the hills.

He kept a firm hold on the rope. "What are you doing here?"

"One of your big oil rigs is down, and they need your advice."

"I've got a cow that needs me right now. The rig's going to have to wait."

"But—"

"The cow's first." He put the rope down and walked toward the truck. He looked every inch a cowboy—tough, rugged, dependable, a man in his element. Mud covered him from black cowboy hat to scuffed boots, and it all looked as if it belonged exactly where it was.

Suddenly her hormones didn't seem to understand that just last night she and Brice had agreed to stay away from each other. And when his smile cut a white crescent through the mud on his face, she wanted nothing more than to kiss that face. He stuck his head in through the window, and she forbid herself to do what she wanted.

He said, "I need your help here, Pru."

She concentrated on his words and not him. "Me help you? Here? Now? Like this?" She glanced down at her suit.

"That's what I had in mind."

"Brice, I'm no cowboy or cowgirl or anything cow. I'm just a messenger. Besides, I'm not exactly dressed for the occasion. I just got home from work, when I got this call for you, and I had to play the loving, caring wife role so everyone would know we're madly in love. After this, I should do Broadway."

He opened the door to his truck. "All you have to do is hold on to the rope around the cow's neck, and when I push her from behind, you guide from in front so she'll know where to go. That way, she'll help herself more and lessen the chances of breaking a leg."

''Sounds muddy.''

''I wouldn't ask if it was muddy.''

''Yes, you would.''

''Well, maybe.''

A pitiful little *moo* suddenly filled the air. Looking some feet away Prudence saw the cutest little brown-and-white calf. ''Her baby?''

''I got the calf out and tied her so she won't go back in the soup after the mother. Now I have to get the mother out. I tried to use Slim—'' Brice nodded toward his horse ''—but being pulled by a horse spooked the cow. Then you came along.'' Brice arched his brow. ''I wouldn't ask but...''

And she knew he wouldn't unless he was desperate. Brice McCormack wasn't a man who asked a lot of favors, except when it came to his cows. Like it or not, she owed him more than delivering a message. He'd not only caught her when the roof gave way, he'd given her a vote of confidence when he handed her those matches. And in return, she had commandeered his truck. Well, darn.

''All you need for me to do is guide from the front, right?''

His grin reached his eyes. ''That's it. It's dry where you'll have to stand. You won't even get your shoes dirty.''

''Good. I can afford to lose only so many shoes in one week.'' Brice held out his muddy hand to help her out of the truck, but she shooed him back with a little wave. ''It's the first time I've worn this suit. It's eggplant, a new power-suit color.''

He grinned hugely. "You look very powerful, Pru."

"Do you want my help or not, McCormack?"

Brice took a few steps back, took his hat off his head and bowed low, as she stepped from the truck. "You have my undying gratitude. But watch where you step. This is cow country, if you know what I mean." Another little *moo* sounded, followed by a louder, forlorn one. She'd been suckered in by two cows and a handsome cowboy. Some city girl she was.

Brice picked up the rope attached to the cow. He handed it to Prudence. It was covered in mud. "Here—" he said, pulling off his work gloves. "These will protect your hands."

Using the two-finger method, Prudence kept her hands away from her suit and slipped on the gloves. They weren't any cleaner than the rope, but she could take off the gloves when she was finished.

"See—" Brice called as he headed back toward the cow. "You and your new power suit will leave here unscathed. Now, when I start to push the cow, she'll try to walk out of the mud. You tug the rope a bit, showing her the way to go. As soon as she's free, just drop the rope. That's all there is to it."

"Got it." Pru's hands felt lost in Brice's heavy leather gloves, but she clamped her fingers tight around the rope, then looped it around a few times so it wouldn't slip out. She carefully pulled in the slack so as not to splash or dislodge anything dirty. Brice waded into the quagmire and trudged his way to the back of the cow. The cow mooed and the calf answered.

This was a good thing she was doing, Prudence reassured herself.

"Okay," Brice called. "On the count of three, pull the rope tight, and I'll push." Brice counted, Pru pulled; the cow mooed and tossed her head, and her baby replied. The cow stumbled and fell to one side. For a moment, Prudence feared Brice might get caught underneath, but then the cow found her footing and staggered out of the mud and onto firm land. Eyeing her calf, she took off in a trot, then a run. Pru watched the grin spread over Brice's face. For a second, time froze.

She'd never seen Brice look so truly happy, and he wasn't happy over oil or money or power or being the head of the McCormacks. He was happy because he'd saved a cow and reunited a mom and baby. Prudence felt her eyes sting with tears and her heart swell with respect for him. No one had ever looked so attractive, so wonderful, so admirable as Brice looked at this very moment.

He was saying something. It seemed to be something important, but the loud mooing and thundering hoofs as the mama cow ran by drowned out his words. He waved, looking a bit frantic. She flashed a victorious smile. Then she heard him yell her name, just a second before there was a hard jerk on her hands that made her stumble. She was yanked around in the other direction, then propelled through the air as if caught in a tornado.

Yikes, she'd forgotten to let go of the blasted rope!

Chapter Seven

Prudence hit the ground with a hard *whamp,* her arms stretched out in front. Her ribs, stomach, hips and knees bounced over the ground, and she felt like some child's pull-toy that had lost its wheels. She fought to keep her head up, as sticks, leaves and mud slid by. She tried to release the rope, but it was tangled in Brice's oversize gloves and pulled tight over her fingers. Her teeth rattled as her head bounced up-down, up-down.

Finally she stopped. Her arms felt as if they'd been pulled from their sockets, but the gushy ground around the pond had spared her from being cut to ribbons. She could hear the happy mooings of mama and baby in front of her. She could also hear Brice frantically calling her name, but she was too winded to answer. A second later the rope holding her arms went slack, and Brice turned her over.

"Pru? Pru? Open your eyes. Say something."

"You owe me a suit."

He exhaled a deep breath. "Why didn't you let go?"

I was too busy realizing what a great guy you are didn't sound like an appropriate answer, especially since less than twenty-four hours ago they'd agreed to avoid each other so they could get on with their lives once this feud ended. Instead, she said, "I was watching the...cows."

"Like hell, you were looking straight at me with some dopey expression on your face. Didn't you hear me yelling at you to let go of the rope?" He did a quick clinical assessment of her limbs. "I don't think anything's broken."

Maybe not—but now she wasn't just unnerved, disoriented and pummeled, she was turned on. How could she be turned on when she couldn't even walk?

"Can you help me sit up?"

He did that, then said, "Looks like you only got a scrape on your nose and one on your chin. Good thing the ground here is soft and...oh, boy." Brice held her shoulders but turned his face away from her and cowered.

"Oh, boy, what?" She blinked a few times to clear the dizziness, and pulled in a few deep breaths. "Criminy, Brice, those cows smell awful." Her eyes teared from the odor. "I never knew cows could smell so bad. Whew!"

Using two fingers, Brice unwound the rope from her gloves and slipped her hands free. He tossed the gloves far over his shoulder, then wiped her face and hair with his bandanna. He tossed that, too. "Pru, honey, it's not the cows that smell."

She was still woozy, and her eyes felt as if they

were rolling around in her head like marbles in an empty box. And that smell was making her sick. "Never figured pond water to smell so bad."

"It doesn't."

"Must be the mud. I didn't notice it driving out here. In fact, I thought it smelled..." Her eyes suddenly focused, and her gaze locked with Brice's. He looked kind, understanding and totally sympathetic.

"Pru, the cattle just went through here and...and where cattle go there's bound to be..."

"Cow poop? I have cow poop on me!" She swiped frantically at her suit. "My hair? Do I have it in my hair?"

"Just a little, sweetheart. It'll wash—"

"Get it out!" She jumped up, pulling wildly at her hair. "Get it out! Get it out!"

"It'll wash out. In four or five shampoos you'll never know—"

Pru yanked off her skirt, jacket, blouse and stockings, tossing them as far away from her as possible, leaving her clad in her teddy, garter belt and panties. They seemed to be clean. At least, they didn't have telltale black smudges of questionable origin on them. Wet grass tickled her toes, and the sun offered some warmth, but she wouldn't have cared if it was forty degrees below zero. Cold beat cow poop any day.

Brice looked dumbstruck, as if he didn't know what to make of her behavior. Then again, how many women did a striptease on a cow path?

The sound of hoofbeats approaching drew her and

Brice's attention down the path she'd follow to get here. It was Derek. No doubt followed by the entire McCormack clan, toting their cameras. Whatever had happened to the lonely life of a cowboy she'd always heard about?

Brice moved in front of her, affording a bit of cover, as Derek pulled up short, keeping a good distance between himself and Brice and Prudence.

"Jumpin' Jehoshaphat," Derek said, his eyes wide, surveying the scattered clothes. "Didn't mean to interrupt anything, big brother. When you didn't show up, I got worried. Hadn't figured on you two being out here and...and..."

Brice shook his head. "Derek, this isn't what you think. Pru got tangled up in a rope and—"

"Hold on, now." Derek's eyes widened more, and he looked away. "Don't want to hear anything about ropes and the like. That's none of my business. I'll just take Slim and the cows and be on my way."

"Look, Derek—" Brice said.

Derek held up his hands as if stopping a charging herd of cattle. "I don't want to look, big brother. Fact is, I don't want any explanations at all." He slid from his saddle and quickly snatched up the ropes. "To think some folks doubted you and Pru actually...well, you know what they doubted. Whoa, were they ever wrong. McCormacks and Randolphs can get along mighty fine, once they set their minds to it. Who would have thought?"

Derek remounted and tied the ropes to his saddle horn. He smiled broadly and tipped his hat. "I'll take care of the cattle and Slim. You two just take care of yourselves, now, you hear. See you later, much later.'' Then he took off, back the way he'd come.

Prudence groaned. ''Stuff like this never happens to me in town. I always have my clothes on in town. What am I doing out here? How could this happen to me? I'm basically a nice person. Don't cheat on my taxes. Give big candy bars to the trick-or-treaters.''

Brice faced her. ''You've had a little run of bad luck, Pru. That's all.''

''A little?'' Was that squeaky voice really hers? He went to touch her, but she backed away, shaking her head. ''I…stink. I've fallen off a roof. I sleep in bags.'' She swallowed a self-pitying sob. ''Get the truck, there's a blanket on the front seat. I had it there to protect my new…'' She eyed her jacket, blouse, skirt and hose. One shoe was half-buried in the mud; heaven knows where the other one was. ''Just get the truck.''

Brice unbuttoned his shirt and held it out to her. ''Take this to keep warm. You're…chilled.''

The sun was dropping fast. Goose bumps covered her arms, and she could feel her nipples tingle against her teddy. Brice would have to be blind not to notice it, too. But considering the other indignities she'd suffered in the past fifteen minutes, stiff nipples didn't even deserve a mention.

BRICE LEANED AGAINST the wall in the back hallway, listening to the shower in the mudroom run full tilt.

He'd brought Pru her shampoo and some other stuff she'd asked for. She'd been in there for a half-hour now. Since he'd grabbed a quick shower upstairs, there couldn't be more than a thimbleful of hot water left by now.

"Pru?" he called through the cracked wood door that separated the mudroom from the hall. He knocked twice. "You okay in there?" He'd been tempted to add *city girl,* but since she'd been introduced to both ends of a cow in rather spectacular ways today, city girl didn't seem to fit. "You're awfully quiet," he called again.

"Cow poop doesn't make me chatty."

"Is it any consolation to know that Derek can't keep a secret to save his soul, and that by now half of Serenity's heard that you and I were in the middle on nowhere having sex with wild abandon. It's got to be good for the Randolph-McCormack image we're aiming for."

"Excuse me if I can't work up any enthusiasm at the moment, but I still smell like cattle dung."

He felt a smile push across his face. It was easy to do that now that Pru was safe in the shower joking about her condition, but he sure hadn't felt like smiling when he'd watched her being dragged across the ground. For the second time in two days, she'd scared the liver out of him.

Steering clear of her wasn't such a great idea, after all. She was completely out of her element on a ranch and needed watching over. He owed her that much. Of course, when they'd been together, his hormones had gone into overdrive. He could still see her standing in the field, wearing that white lace teddy—with a hint of nipple showing—surrounded by springtime and sunshine. The little rose tattoo on her thigh still upped Brice's blood pressure a good ten points. Pru's current fragrance may not have been designer quality, but everything else about her was damn fine.

In fact, just knowing she was in the shower right now, naked as a jaybird, gave him heart palpitations. He shifted his weight from one foot to the other, hoping to find a more comfortable position. It did no good.

The door to the mudroom opened, and Pru stood in front of him wrapped in a fluffy white towel that only reached mid-thigh. A cloud of steam surrounded her, and her lashes were spiked from the water, framing her deep blue eyes. Droplets trickled down her face, neck and chest, disappearing into the hint of cleavage. She still didn't look very happy, but she didn't look too upset, either.

She said, "Good, you're here." She looked up at him, making his breath catch in his throat. Her tongue caught a drop of water that had been clinging to her top lip, and his insides fired hotter than a branding iron at roundup time. "I need your help." Her eyes narrowed for a moment, and she asked, "You did call your oil rig people, didn't you?"

"Everything's taken care of. Thanks."

"You're welcome. Now I need you to help me." She stuck the top of her head in his face. "Does it still smell like...like you-know-what?"

Brice stared at the mass of damp, springy auburn curls in front of him. He wanted to run his hands through her hair, dry her wet face and snap that towel right off her body. The scent of warm vanilla filled his lungs and swirled around him, bewitching him like some voodoo spell.

"You smell great, Pru. Wonderful, magnificent."

She kept her head down and asked, "No cow? You're sure, absolutely sure?"

He pulled in every ounce of self-control he possessed and stuffed his hands in his pockets to make sure they didn't do any towel snapping. "Yeah, I'm absolutely sure. And I'm really sorry about all this."

Right now, he was sorrier than he could tell her. If she hadn't come after him, none of this would be happening, and the two of them would still be avoiding each other.

Then again, she did help him save the cow. He owed her for that. "I'll make this up to you, Pru. I'll have my men work the two-track into a drivable lane. You can have your Lincoln back, and you don't ever have to ride in a truck again."

She raised her head and gave him a smile that lit up her face like sun on snow. "Thank you."

Those two words along with her incredible smile crumpled his self-control. How could he stay away from someone so lovely, so giving, so understanding of the responsibilities he faced?

He kissed her because he'd been dying to all day, and because in so many ways she was his soul mate. She was unlike any other woman he'd ever met.

They'd been interested in what he and his money could do for them. Not Pru. She understood responsibility and family obligations and the demands both made on him, and she helped when she didn't have to at all.

He cupped her face, savoring the warmth of her soft skin against his rough palms, remembering the whimpers she'd made deep in her throat when he'd kissed her. She seemed so delicate, almost fragile, yet she had incredible inner strength. Her body leaned in to his, and he inhaled her unique feminine scent as their tongues stroked and caressed. He was on fire for her, and every muscle in his body was rock hard.

God, he wanted her! He ran his hands down her elegant throat, over her shoulders and down her arms, which curved in front of her. She was holding the towel, and when he considered what was under that towel, his blood boiled like coffee on a campfire.

"I want you to make love to me, Brice. I want to make love to you."

He gritted his teeth as his body throbbed. Hearing her admit what he felt was a powerful aphrodisiac.

"We can't be true to each other *and* to our families, Pru. Making love isn't going to change who we are."

"Then…we'll be someone else. We'll escape. Forget who we are." She tipped her head and gave him a hot sultry look that was not at all like the Pru he knew. "Hi, my name's Prudence…Smith."

"Smith?"

"Uh-huh. And you're Brice...Jones."

He laughed. "This is nuts."

"It's the only thing I can come up with on short notice."

"Oh, boy." He grimaced. "We have a problem."

"Brice, we have lots of problems. You'll have to be more specific."

"I don't have...protection."

Pru let out a long, hot breath and rested her forehead against his chin. "Ms. Smith is going to go take a very cold shower before she combusts."

Pru felt wonderful in his arms, all warm and soft with wanting him. "Wait."

"Wait?" She gazed up at him. Her eyes opened wide and the pulse at the base of her throat beat faster than lightning strikes on a summer night.

"In my luggage upstairs. I might—"

She pressed her fingers to his lips. "Hurry."

"If I'm not back in a minute, go take that shower."

PRUDENCE LISTENED to the sound of Brice's boots on the wood floors, echoing through the nearly empty house. She could hear him moving around upstairs, and her insides burned with anticipation. His rapid footfalls sounded on the steps again, making her hopes soar—until she saw him bolt out the front door, taking all hopes of lovemaking right along with him. This was not turning out to be one of her better days. She'd had a lot of those lately, she realized as she headed for the shower.

The cold water felt like ice pellets pummeling her skin. Closing her eyes, she reasoned that her current situation was meant to be. She and Brice should not get involved. They were compatible, but they certainly didn't trust each other. All they needed to do was hang together to end the feud, then they'd go back to being heads of their families. Making love would just add more confusion to an already confusing relationship, though she'd give her Lincoln for some of Brice's "physical confusion" right now.

Suddenly, she heard Brice quietly say her name. She opened her eyes, pulled back the shower curtain and saw him standing in the mudroom. He was as naked as she was, and he looked magnificent. No man had a right to be so trim, so muscled, so...so very well-endowed. Her insides turned to jelly, except for a spot deep inside that blazed hot and wild. The hot part she'd felt before, but never, ever the wild.

Keeping his eyes on her, Brice walked over and switched the water to warm, then slid into the tiny shower with her. She watched his thick black hair mat to his scalp and droplets run down his face and off his chin. She swiped his hair from his forehead, noticing a scorching heat gleaming in his eyes.

He said, "Ms. Smith, you are gorgeous. Perfect. Incredible. Sexy as hell."

"Mr. Jones, if you don't have a condom, you're dead meat."

A grin cut across his face, and he winked. "In Derek's truck, buried under a pile of stuff in the glove compartment.'' He held the faded, crinkled-up gold package in the palm of his hand for her to see.

Desire whirled through her. ''I want to go to bed with you, Brice.'' He was a delicious-looking man, all cowboy and, right now, all hers. Her fingers trailed down his arms and across his chest, running through his short dark hair. His erection pressed hard between her hips, making her dizzy with anticipation.

''Pru, we don't have a bed.'' This made her laugh. Then he kissed her hard, sending shivers up her spine in spite of the warm water. He balanced the little gold package on top of her shampoo bottle, then gently cupped her breasts, running the pad of his thumb over her nipples, sending tremors through her body. ''Do you like that, Pru?'' His eyes darkened to the color of chocolate.

Her voice failed her completely, and she was reduced to nodding. She ran her hands over his stomach, then below. He sucked in a quick breath as she held him, teased him, memorized the feel of him in her hands. His fingers slid down her sides, across her thighs. Tenderly, he opened her legs.

She thought she was prepared for him to touch her, but when his fingers connected with her most feminine spot, she nearly dissolved and slid down the drain. Desire burned in his eyes as she reached for the condom, tore it open and slowly, deliberately, provocatively covered him. His breathing quickened, and the pulse at his temple beat a rapid tattoo.

''Put your hands on my shoulders, sweetheart. When I lift you up, just wrap your legs around me.''

She closed her eyes, but he said, ''No, Pru. I want you to watch me. I want to see our lovemaking in your eyes.''

The passion and hunger in his voice and on his face thrilled her, excited her as she had never been before. And when he cupped her derriere and lifted her, letting the wall support her back, she knew she wanted Brice more than she wanted anything else on earth.

Instinctively she encircled his hips with her legs and welcomed him inside her.

BRICE SLOWLY entered her. He wanted to relish their lovemaking, letting her adjust to the feel of him bit by bit, and he luxuriated in the warm, wet feel of her. He leaned her back against the wall, giving her more control. He wanted to treasure the fevered look on her face as they joined as one, as he possessed her and she certainly possessed him. ''Easy,'' he coaxed, as she tightened her legs around him.

Her breasts rose and fell with the rapid rhythm of her breath. Her eyes darkened to sapphire and dilated. Her hands gripped his shoulders till her knuckles blanched white. ''Brice?''

''Just let it happen, sweetheart.'' He kissed her, tasting passion on her lips, her tongue, in her mouth. Intense heat ran through him like a range fire destroying everything in its path. Control gave way to obsession, and he pushed into her, sending them both into total ecstasy. He called her name, yelled it, heard his voice mix with hers, echoing off the shower walls. Never had he felt more complete, more satisfied than he did at this moment, loving Pru.

Pru sagged against him, meshing their bodies. He kissed her neck, her ear, her hair. Suddenly he realized the water pouring over them was ice cold. "Hold on to me, sweetheart." Brice wrapped his arms around her tightly and stepped out of the water. Slowly, he set her down on the old concrete floor, enfolded her in her towel, then disposed of the condom.

"Here—" she said when he came back to her, opening her arms to welcome him into her towel, her warmth. The expression on her face and in her blue eyes was happiness, joy, contentment. He'd never seen her look that way before, and realized he'd caused it—it was very addictive, indeed.

She wrapped her arms and the towel around his shoulders, snuggling against him. The feel of her so close, so loving was incredible.

"Brice—"

He felt her breath on his lips.

"We're not doing a very good job of staying away from each other."

"I don't want to stay away, Pru." He watched her eyes sparkle in agreement, and he felt happier than he'd ever have thought possible. "I want to give what we feel for each other a chance. But that's not going to happen until our families stop battling, and we can concentrate on each other instead of them." Brice gave her a thoughtful look. "Before, I wanted to end the feud so we could get out of our marriage.

Now, I want to end the feud to see if there's any chance of saving it.''

''For years, no one's been able to make any progress toward getting the families together, Brice. That's not very encouraging.'' She let out a long, dejected-sounding sigh.

''That's because there's been a lack of proper motivation.'' He kissed the tip of her nose. ''I want to make love with you again and again. I want us to be close. I want us to be able to trust each other. I want us to be the best of friends, on fire for each other with nothing in the way. We can't get to that stage until we solve our problems, and we can't do that until we solve the problems between our families.'' He stole another quick kiss, then said, ''Right now, we happen to be the two most motivated people on planet Earth to put an end to this blasted feud.''

PRUDENCE TRIED NOT TO THINK about how she and Brice had made love only three hours ago and how she wanted to make love with him again, right now. Instead, she concentrated on the page of notes she'd taken as they shared a picnic dinner in front of the hearth—a dinner the two of them had cooked on their new stove—and tried to think of ways to end the feud. Sunny had told her that a common cause pulls people together, so she and Brice were now racking their brains to come up with some cause. It was a mighty poor substitute for what she wanted to do, but it was very necessary.

Brice stretched his legs out on the blanket and

leaned against the raised stone. Firelight danced in his hair and gave a warm glow to his tanned face. Her concentration waned. How in Hades was she supposed to come up with ways of ending anything at all, when it took every ounce of fortitude she possessed *not* to persuade him to make love to her. A mental image of the persuading part sent little shivers of anticipation through her; it presented great possibilities. But it was out of the question because they were out of protection. Bringing a baby into the middle of this feud was not an option.

"Okay," Brice said, yanking her away from her lusty thoughts. "Read the suggestions we've come up with so far to bring the two most hardheaded families in North America together."

"We have the great chili cook-off, the town beautification project, paint and fix up the library, have a book drive, put in a playground for the kids, build a baseball field, construct a shelter at Pine Tree Ridge, have a rodeo."

Brice picked up his fifth piece of fried chicken from the plate and helped himself to a fourth helping of pasta salad. If she ate like that she'd look like a blimp, she thought. Brice was no blimp. How could he pack away so much food and keep so fit? And he was indeed fit. Her blood hummed in her veins just thinking about his fitness. Good thing she'd bought the best stove and biggest fridge she could find in town. Cooking was about to become more than just a passing hobby in the Randolph-McCormack house.

Brice took a bite of chicken. Around a mouthful of food he said, "Which ideas do you like best?"

She tapped her pencil against the paper. "Hmm. The chili cook-off might be too competitive. I see fistfights and bloodshed over that one, since chili is serious business in Texas." She ran her pen through that suggestion. "The town beautification project is mostly a Randolph thing, since we live in town and your family lives in the boonies. What do you think?"

"I think this isn't the boonies. We like to think of it as the wide-open spaces. But the rodeo is a McCormack thing." Brice gave Prudence a cocky smile that made her heart skip a beat. "The Randolphs wouldn't have a chance at that one."

"True. Just like if we had a competition on who could fill out their own tax returns, the McCormacks wouldn't have a chance there." She gave Brice a smug grin.

"Point taken." She ran her pen through the words *beautification project* and *rodeo.* But she would have loved to see Brice at a rodeo.

He continued, "We need something neutral, but not the library. If anything goes wrong, I'd rather keep books and periodicals out of harm's way."

Prudence scratched off the library idea and looked back to the list. "That leaves us with a baseball field, a playground and a shelter." She tapped her pencil on the pad again. "What if we put in a baseball field, playground and shelter at Pine Tree Ridge? That covers a lot of interests. Both families, plus everybody else in town, especially the kids, use it for picnics, baseball, soccer, hikes. It wouldn't be seen as favoring one family over the other. It's always been kind of detached from the feuding. Fixing it up would benefit everyone. It would be a philanthropic project for both families that neither could find fault with."

"Whoa, that's a considerable undertaking, Pru. We'd have to do it in stages. But you're right about one thing—it is neutral territory. Not neutral like the ranch here because we're both owners, but neutral all the same, and that's the important thing."

Had he really said "both owners" without hesitating or blinking an eye? Fatigue had obviously robbed him of his good sense. Or maybe it was kissing her that had lowered his defenses to an all-time low. She hoped so. Ending this feud was one heck of a lot more complicated than keeping it going.

"The question is, how in blazes are we going to get both families to show up at the same place, and convince them to use shovels, saws and hammers on a building and not on each other?" He looked her dead in the eyes. "If we can solve that little dilemma, Pru, we can solve damn near anything."

Chapter Eight

''We'll lie,'' Prudence said, after swallowing a mouthful of potato salad and washing it down with lemonade. ''With all we've been through in trying to keep our families out of the county jail, we're pros at lying, whether we like it or not.'' She paused, then added, ''We'll use some basic principles of feud psychology.''

''*What* kind of psychology?''

''The kind where you just happen to mention to your family that the Randolphs are putting up a shelter at Pine Tree Ridge. Then you throw in the clincher. You tell them the Randolphs are doing this for the town, and the town's putting up a big plaque with the Randolph name on it. You casually say something like, 'It's a rotten shame the McCormack family is getting outdone by the Randolphs.' *Plaque* and *outdone* are the critical words, here, believe me. Then offhandedly maybe suggest that the McCormacks build sandboxes, swings and picnic tables. Whenever one family hears that the other is doing something the first is not, it stampedes into immediate action. 'Course, I'll tell my family the opposite story. Everyone will show up on the same day because they'll want to keep an eye on what the other's doing. We'll get the judge to donate two plaques, and the town gets a great park in the bargain. *Voilà!* Feud psychology in action.'' She gave herself a mental pat on the back for coming up with such a great scheme.

For a second, Brice looked overwhelmed by what she'd said, then replied, ''It's worth a try, since we haven't come up with anything else. We should aim for Sunday.''

''This Sunday?''

''No reason to wait, and the sooner we solve our families' problems, the sooner we can concentrate on our own.''

She suddenly felt all warm and wonderful inside, just thinking that she and Brice could possibly have a future together. Suddenly, she couldn't imagine her future without him. ''Can we pull everything together that fast? I mean, this will take some planning.''

For a moment Brice seemed lost in thought, the crackle of burning logs, and the creaks and moans of an old house the only sounds. A faint scent of smoke hung in the air, and moonlight sliced through the windows, forming rectangles on the worn wood floor. Prudence wondered about the Dillards and others who had sat in front of this hearth, all nice and cozy and making plans about their lives. This house might be dilapidated now, but at one time it was a good house, she could feel it. If it could talk, it would probably have some great tales to tell.

Brice finally said, ''Since keeping things peaceful is our main objective here, we need to provide the food. No potluck dinners. If anyone said there was better fried chicken than Aunt Lilly's, the feud would have no chance of ending for another seventy years.''

''I can cook, and get Sunny to help.''

''I'll figure out how much lumber, nails, screws and roofing materials we'll need. I'll order those things in town tomorrow and arrange for delivery. But let's wait till Friday to spring this idea on our families. Giving them short notice cuts down on their trouble-planning time.''

Prudence looked Brice dead in the eyes. ''Our wedding was on short notice. Remember? Look what happened there.''

''Then we're overdue for a success, Pru.'' Brice winked and grinned.

Oh, boy! What that man did to her hormones with one smile was...sinful. She watched him stretch out on the blanket and cup his hands behind his head as he stared at the cracked ceiling.

He said, ''You and me sitting here, calmly working on the same idea to settle family problems, is as strange as snow in July. If anyone had told me a week ago that we could do this without winding up in a yelling match or in court, I would have thought they were off their rocker.''

Prudence snatched some pinecones from the pile of kindling and absently tossed them into the fire, watching them burst into flames. She'd never felt so peaceful, so content, as she did at this moment. Maybe it was being out here where there was nothing but trees and grass and cows and this run-down house. All this quiet and simplicity gave her time to consider who she really was. Concrete and traffic, she realized, weren't conducive to self-exploration.

She said, "Being with you sure takes the pressure off me, I can tell you that. For once in my life, I don't have to listen to Dad go on about what the great Brice McCormack is doing over at the Half-Circle, and then have to figure out how I am going to match it."

His gaze cut to her. "What the heck's that supposed to mean?"

Pru watched another pinecone catch fire, and the scent of deep forest filled the room. "Don't you know 'Randolphs have to keep up with McCormacks.' At least, that's what Dad says. And that means I have to keep up with you." This time she tossed a pinecone onto his chest. "In case you didn't know, Brice McCormack, keeping up with you is a royal pain in the hind end. Only this time I don't have to keep up with you because I'm here, too. As Aunt Patty says, 'God works in mysterious ways.'"

"You're kidding, right?"

"Heck, no, God really does work—"

"Not that." He sat up. "The part about keeping up with me."

She pitched in the last pinecone, then drew her legs up, wrapping her arms around her knees.

"Didn't it ever occur to you just why I was yearbook editor when you were editor of the newspaper? Or why we won so many of the same honors in high school? Or what in Sam Hill I was doing at Pine Tree Ridge with the Scouts the very week you got an Eagle Scout award?"

"Your dad made you do what I did?"

"Not *made,* exactly. More like…expected, since I was his daughter and next in line to Bob Randolph, grand pooh-bah of the Randolph family. In high school I used to send telepathic thoughts your way. Thoughts like 'Brice, take an art class. Brice, take a cooking class. Brice, learn to play the piano.' But did you? Ha! Once I even slipped a newspaper article in your gym locker about how ballet classes helped football players improve their coordination and kicking skills."

"I remember seeing that. Hey, it worked."

Her jaw dropped. "You took ballet lessons? And I didn't know about it? Is there any justice in this world?"

"I paid Derek a month's allowance to keep that quiet."

"Couldn't you have paid him to keep your taking calculus quiet, instead? I hated calculus, but since you took it, guess who had to take it, too?" She shrugged and let go of her knees, then reached for the paper plates they'd used. "It's getting late—we better clean this up and get some sleep. We've got a busy few days ahead of us, if we're going to pull off this Pine Tree Ridge plan."

Unexpectedly, Brice placed his hand on hers, and she looked at him, their gazes connecting and holding. Concern covered his face. "I'm sorry, Pru. I really am."

"What for?"

"For...for taking calculus. I never knew that anything I did affected you. I've just done whatever I had to for the sake of the family. I knew that one day the responsibility of running the Half-Circle would be mine, and the family would depend on me to make it a success. I had to be prepared, and if that meant taking calculus and being a business major, I had to do it."

She turned her hand palm up and took hold of his. His hands were hard and callused and totally dependable. "You took charge of the Half-Circle when other young men were footloose and fancy-free, Brice. You grew up in a hurry when your dad died. All the responsibility fell to you. You've made this ranch bigger and better than ever. You did it because you had to, and everyone admires you for it." She gave him a soft smile. "Even me."

"Don't make me out to be some hero, Pru. I'm not."

She cupped his chin with her fingers. His stubble prickled her hand, his eyes dark as the coals in the grate. "The only thing stopping you from being perfect, cowboy, is that you're not a Randolph."

His smile joined hers. "I'll keep that in mind." Then he kissed her lightly on the cheek.

A kiss on the cheek was not exactly the sort of

kiss Pru wanted from him. There were a lot more interesting places she could suggest he kiss. But they both knew that making love tonight was out of the question. Finding that one tattered-looking foil pouch buried in Derek's truck had been a stroke of luck that wasn't going to repeat itself.

Tonight was going to be a really long one, with Brice in one sleeping bag and her in another. But tomorrow… Ah, tomorrow would be another story.

BRICE PARKED the pickup in one of the white-lined diagonal spaces in front of the courthouse. He looked at the wide porch, and for a moment remembered the day when Judge Willis had decreed he and Pru get married, or else. Then the two of them had sat there and desperately tried to figure a way out of the mess they were in. He was glad they hadn't.

Pru's soft skin, delicious lips, lovely blue eyes and rose tattoo were great distractions from normal McCormack business. And making love to her was a distraction beyond his wildest dreams. Discovering the real Prudence Randolph was the most surprising thing of all.

He'd always known she was an exceptional woman, a take-charge kind of person who shouldered more than her share of responsibility. But when she took on fixing up the Dillard house instead of insisting they move back into town, and then helped him with the cow, he'd been completely amazed.

How could Bob Randolph have coerced Pru into being Brice's clone, when she had so many wonderful qualities of her own? Didn't Randolph appreciate just how remarkable she truly was? Brice always suspected that when it came to common sense, the Randolphs—except for Pru—weren't the sharpest knives in the drawer. The way Bob Randolph treated his only daughter proved hands-down that Brice was right.

He caught sight of Derek coming out of the courthouse, heading for the steps. "Hey," Brice yelled from his open truck window. He waved, then left the truck and fell into step beside Derek on the sidewalk. "Just the guy I need to see."

"Here to give me a progress report on how *my* truck's running?"

"Not exactly, little brother. But it is as fine as bug dust."

"Any idea just when I'm going to get my fine-as-bug-dust truck back?"

"Real soon, now. Real soon. I'm just borrowing it for a spell, and you can use one of the extra ranch trucks until I do."

"Brice, they all smell like cow."

"Yeah, I know. That's why I snatched yours and not one of them." Brice laughed, and Derek rolled his eyes. "So," Brice continued, "what brings you to town? Thought you were heading out to brand cattle on the south pasture today."

"Uncle Judd and his boys rode out there this morning. I'm stuck here running errands with Granddad Wes. Hope we don't meet up with Eulah. Every time those two run into each other, all hell breaks loose. It's mighty strange. Almost like they enjoy getting together, but then they battle like wolves over a carcass."

"You're errand running? Since when?"

"Since Granddad's still in a state over you marrying Prudence, and Mama wants me to keep him out of everyone's hair until he gets over it—which is looking like next to never."

Brice set his hat back on his head. "That's not what I want to hear. Pru and I are racking our brains, trying to find ways to bring the families together. You know, stop the bickering so we can have some kind of peace in our lives and in this town."

"I think you and Pru might be the only ones in that frame of mind. I sure don't see anyone else in either family trying to bring the Randolphs and McCormacks together, and your marriage has done zilch to improve the situation. Though people are plumb amazed you two are getting along."

"Tell me, what's your opinion of getting both families to work on a shelter at Pine Tree Ridge?"

Derek stopped dead in his tracks, then laughed.

"Now, just think about this for a minute before you go off half-cocked. Everyone in town uses Pine Tree Ridge. The McCormacks and Randolphs are civic-minded families. Don't you think there's a chance they'd work together on this project?"

"About as much chance as a hothouse surviving a hailstorm. The only thing your idea has going for it is that Pine Tree Ridge is about fifty acres in size, giving everyone plenty of room for fighting and—"

"No more fighting, that's the whole point. If we could get a few people, maybe even *one* person, to cooperate in this plan we have, it would be more than we had a week ago." Brice gave Derek a meaningful look. "Just one person, little brother."

"Me?" Derek's eyes widened, and he poked his own chest. "You want *me* to get along with the Randolphs?"

"Pru said how nice you were to her, and that you wanted to come for dinner and all."

"That was just showboating. Besides, dinner with you and Pru isn't like getting chummy with *all* the Randolphs."

Brice stuffed his hands into his jeans pockets. "Okay, little brother, let's cut to the chase, here. What's it going to take for you to get neighborly with the Randolphs? Name your price—and I know you have a price."

"I get my truck back."

"I can do that."

"And you pay for new tires. Those oversize ones with white lettering."

Brice pulled in a breath. "I can spring for the tires with lettering."

"Well, doggies." Derek brother-punched Brice. "This is working out real good. I've had my eye on Sally Randolph for some time and just couldn't figure out a way of meeting up with her. Since you and Prudence have got this shindig cooked up, now it'll be easy as shooting fish in a barrel to spend some time with her. Thanks, Brice."

"What happened to that bit about not wanting to get along with the Randolphs, huh?"

"Hey, I smelled an opportunity heading my way, that's all." Derek gave Brice a cheeky grin. "Always hold out for the best offer is what you've taught me, and you're one heck of a good teacher."

"Yay for me."

"Besides, you ran off with my truck. You owe me." Derek folded his arms across his chest and looked smug as a bull at breeding time.

"Since you're so all-fired good at getting your way, what are the chances of you persuading your cousins to be neighborly to the Randolphs, too?"

"Now, that there's a tall order." Derek stroked his chin and half closed his eyes in thought. It was the look of someone who knew he had the upper hand and was enjoying it immensely. "My truck would kick butt if it had a sunroof, and maybe a CD player. Always wanted a CD player with heavy bass. Bet Sally Randolph would be mighty impressed with a sunroof and CD player."

Brice ground his teeth. "For one sunroof and one CD player, you better do some serious talking to your cousins. But you're not to breathe one word till Friday."

Derek grinned. "Consider it done."

Brice watched Derek cross the street and head over to Boots and Saddles Country. Maybe now that he got Derek and the cousins on his side, the Pine Tree Ridge idea would work. At least, it had a chance. If Pru could get some help with her family, the odds of Randolphs and McCormacks at least tolerating each other would be at its best in seventy years. Not bad, not bad at all.

Brice crossed the street, heading toward Hoof and Hardware to see about nails and fittings to make the shelter, picnic tables and play equipment. He would stop at the lumberyard on his way home and get things lined up there. Hmm, he was actually starting to think of the Dillard place as home. Or was he starting to think of *Pru* as home?

When he reached the sidewalk, he spotted Bob Randolph coming toward him, a scowl plastered on his face. Pru's dad didn't look any more reconciled to his daughter marrying Brice than was Granddad Wes. What would ever make them change?

"Randolph." Brice greeted him.

"McCormack. I want to know what in tarnation you've done with my Prudence."

"What I've done—"

"She's not at work today. No doubt you've got her hog-tied up somewhere, keeping her—"

"Hold on a minute, now. First off, I don't hog-tie women. If Pru isn't at work, she must have a good reason. Didn't she call?"

"'Course she called. Handed me some cock-and-bull story about needing to wait for furniture being delivered, and varnishing the kitchen cabinets while she was waiting." Bob's face turned deep red. "You got my Prudence varnishing for you and doing your fetching and carrying, and I won't have it, you understand. That girl's the apple of my eye, my whole life, my dearest treasure on earth." He poked Brice in the chest. "And you're—"

"Did you ever tell Pru that?"

Bob Randolph's finger stopped mid-poke. "Huh? Tell her what?"

"Tell her just what you told me."

"Prudence knows how I feel about her. She doesn't need to be told."

"Randolph." Brice glared. It was the kind of glare he used in business dealings when someone in a fancy suit tried to pull a fast one on him. "Tell her. She needs to be told. She needs to know her father appreciates her."

"Don't you try to tell me what to say to my own daughter."

Brice's glare hardened just a touch. "I *am* telling you. 'Bout time someone did." Brice turned and left Bob standing in the middle of the sidewalk, yelling something about Prudence being a Randolph, and how no McCormack was going to tell Randolphs how to live their lives.

Brice decided he shouldn't have wasted his breath confronting Bob Randolph. It wouldn't do any good. Randolph wasn't about to change his ways. And even if Brice told Pru all the great things her dad had just said about her, it wasn't nearly as meaningful as if she heard it from her father directly.

There was nothing Brice could do about Bob Randolph and his pigheaded attitude, but Brice could follow his own advice. No matter what happened between him and Pru from here on out, he'd always remember that she'd been a real trooper through some pretty dismal times. Not only had she taken on fixing up the old house, but also she'd taken on some of his problems. He'd also remember Prudence Randolph made the best darn fried chicken he'd ever put in his mouth.

He wasn't going to be like Bob Randolph and assume Pru knew he appreciated all these things about her. He intended to tell her, as soon as he got back to the ranch.

PRUDENCE GOT BACK IN Brice's truck and waved goodbye to Sunny, who stood in the doorway of her house. As Prudence headed out the circular drive and back to the main road, she thought over the plan she and Sunny had concocted this afternoon, after deciding on the picnic menu.

Sunny, who was the president of Serenity's Garden Society, thought it might help if the membership planted deciduous bushes, trees and flowers at Pine Tree Ridge on Sunday. She reasoned that if more people than the McCormacks and Randolphs showed up for the get-together and took part, there was a better chance of keeping confrontations to a minimum. Also, the families wouldn't be so tempted to tear the hell out of the place if there was an audience present who had put in a lot of work to make things look nice.

Prudence smiled to herself. The Pine Tree Ridge plan was coming along just fine. If Randolphs and McCormacks could be civil for a few hours, that would be wonderful, a definite breakthrough, a marked ending to the feud and a beginning for her and Brice.

She had never felt about another man the way she felt about Brice. Oh, she'd dated guys, even went steady with Chase Billows for a year in college. That had ended when they graduated, and their careers and families were more important than their relationship. But now, it was different. Was there anything more important than Brice?

She did know that no one she'd ever met came close to being the man, the cowboy, that Brice McCormack was. He was truly a hero—her hero—for saving her on the roof, and for encouraging her to light that fire. Most guys she'd met wouldn't have cared one way or the other. But Brice did. He was…sensitive—that was a real surprise. And the fact that he wasn't a Randolph didn't matter diddly.

When Prudence turned onto the two-track, she saw that the workmen—along with all their pounding, sawing and sanding—were gone for the day. But the dusty Lincoln with the RR-1 license plate was parked at the front of the house. Her father was waiting for her. A groan crept up her throat and slipped out through clenched teeth. Her insides knotted. She wasn't up to another confrontation with her father right now, and she was sure that's what this was all about. He'd want her to go home with him, probably give her a list of reasons. Then he'd demand that she leave with him, because she was a Randolph and that's what was expected of her.

She couldn't go, of course. Make that *she wouldn't go.* It had nothing to do with Judge Willis's marriage edict or the feud, or the fact that her relatives could end up in jail. The simple truth was, she didn't want to go home...because she was already there.

"Prudence, I need to talk to you," her father said, after she got out and closed the truck door behind her.

He'd obviously been waiting for her for a while. This was very bad. He'd had time to prepare his case. Bob Randolph was excellent at preparing arguments that got people to think the way he did. He was a natural-born litigater if there ever was one.

He said, "I need—"

"Dad, I know you need help since I'm not around as much right now. Uncle Ralph's son passed the bar last week. He's a tax attorney. He's bright and able, much better at taxes than I am, and he can't wait to start—"

"I don't give a hang about the taxes. It's that dang-blasted husband of yours. I ran into him in town." Her dad's face was flushed. He yanked his perfectly knotted silk tie loose from his perfectly starched white shirt, letting the tie hang crookedly around his neck. Heavens to Betsy, what did Brice say to make her dad look like this?

"Dad, Brice is under a lot of stress. You're under a lot of stress. You have to cut each other some slack."

"Stress is no blamed excuse for what he did. That...that man you up and married against my better judgment is a horse's behind, a nincompoop, a total idiot. He had the gall to suggest that you don't know you're the apple of my eye and the best child a father could want.''

She backed up till she connected with the truck, and held on to it for support. Her brain felt fuzzy. ''I...I am?''

''Well, confound it, of course you are, and for that addle-brained McCormack cowboy to suggest you don't know it is an outrage. Though, I must say, he does seem to like you well enough. I'll give him credit for having good taste in that department. Anyway, I just wanted you to understand what kind of man you're married to.''

''I think I do. Thanks for watching out for me, and thanks for coming all the way out here.''

''I'm heading on home now. Just wanted to make sure you're all right and to tell you our back door's open when you come to your senses and leave this hovel McCormack's got you staying in. I intend to protect you, Prudence, since you don't seem to be in your right mind these days. You are my daughter and a Randolph and the future head of the Randolph family.''

''I don't need protecting, Dad. Brice and I are doing fine. Didn't you notice that the front porch is coming along real nice, and the stone chimney's being remortared? Look at that pile of shingles—'' She pointed to the stack by the scaffold. ''We'll have a new roof by next week. And I'm having a bay window installed.''

"Humph. It's still a McCormack dump."

"It's *my* dump, Dad. Brice deeded it to me, remember?"

"Be careful of him, girl. I mean it, now."

She watched her father walk toward his car. He cared. He really, really cared. Beyond family and obligation, he cared what happened to her personally, as his daughter. Deep down, she had suspected as much, but she'd never felt positive until this very minute. "Wait. Wait a minute."

She ran over to him and kissed him on the cheek. "You're a pretty great dad. You know that? In fact, you're an excellent dad." She hugged him for all she was worth. And right now, that felt like quite a lot.

A very untypical cockeyed smile covered her dad's face. Then he winked at Prudence, which was not like her dad, either. He got in his car and drove off, and Prudence watched the dust from the two-track follow the Lincoln as it bumped its way in retreat.

Her eyes welled with tears and a lump lodged in her throat. She sniffed and swiped the back of her hand across her runny nose. "Well, Brice McCormack, you had to go stick your nose in where it didn't belong, didn't you." She sniffed again. "Just wait till you get home."

SHE DIDN'T have long to wait before she heard Brice calling her name as he tramped up the stairs. "Pru? Where are you?"

"In here." She fluffed the pillow and dropped it

on top of the yellow cotton sheet she'd just smoothed over the new mattress.

"Pru," he called as he made his way toward her, "I like that new floor lamp and leather couch. It looks like the Ross clan rewired most of the downstairs and the new windows— Whoa." He stopped in the doorway. "Now, what do we have here?"

She gave him a quick glance. His jeans were clean, his shirt pressed, his boots free of mud splotches. Her heartbeat kicked up two notches just at the sight of him. Either he'd been in town on business, or he'd managed to teach those cows of his some manners about getting people dirty. His hands were behind his back, and a secret smile played on his lips. Ah, those lips, that smile. What was her cowboy up to now? She liked that "her cowboy" part a lot.

She fluffed another pillow and said, "I know we've been without one of these newfangled contraptions for a while, cowboy, but this here is what's called a bed. A brass, queen-size, pillow-top mattress bed. It has no similarities to a sleeping bag whatsoever, and I should tell you that most people consider that a very good thing."

He grinned. "You've really cleaned this place up. What did you do with all the boxes of stuff that were in here?"

She nodded toward the corner. "I went through them. Tossed some in the trash and kept some of the good finds for the Garden Society's annual Button and Bows Vintage Sale. I found some old spurs you might like, and there are a ton of books in the closet that I haven't gotten to.'' She stopped and looked at Brice. ''Did you know Grandma Eulah stayed here with the Dillards for a while? She left behind some books and letters from her parents, who were traveling in Europe. They're in a little box. Thought I'd run them over to her later on. They're almost forty years old—they've got to bring back some memories for her.''

''Probably some bad memories, too, living so close to Wes. Can't imagine those two ever getting along. There must have been some mighty tall fighting and squabbling when they laid eyes on each other, with her living so close by. Just getting them within a hundred feet of each other now is like throwing a match on dry leaves.''

Brice stroked his chin. ''Tell me, Pru, are more beds on the way?''

''This is it for right now. I decided ordering another bed could give the gossips in town the idea there's a need for more beds at the Randolph-McCormack house.'' She returned to fluffing the pillows. ''That's not the impression we want to create. Newlyweds only have one bed on their minds.'' She glanced at him again. ''Do you have a problem with that?'' She put down the pillow and looked directly at him. ''Do *we* have a problem with that?''

''Problem? With just one bed? Hell, I think it's pretty damn terrific.''

''I'm serious, Brice.''

''Oh, sweetheart, so am I.''

Her stomach flipped, but she forced herself to

think of their predicament. "Brice, there's more to this than just sleeping together. What if we can't figure out a way to end the feud? What if the families never see eye-to-eye? If they don't get along, we'll never be able to work things out, because we're committed to them till someone shovels dirt on our graves. Do you think we should start something between us that we may never be able to finish?"

"It's already started, Pru." He leaned against the door frame, looking sexy as all get-out. "Remember in *Casablanca* when Bogie told Ingrid they'd 'always have Paris'? Well, you and I will always have the brass bed."

"I'm trying to be serious, here."

His eyes darkened a shade, and his smile faded. "Let's not. For once in our very structured, planned, responsibility-driven lives, let's not. Family circumstances got us into this—it's our right to enjoy it while we can. And if Lady Luck smiles our way, we'll end this damn feud and sleep in this bed for the rest of our lives." He shrugged. "Besides, I don't think you should have to sleep on the hard floor in the sleeping bag, when I'm up here all warm and comfortable."

He ducked when she flung the pillow at him. "Hey, careful there. I bring presents."

"What kind of presents? Chili fries? Hot wings?"

"All day I was thinking about getting you a new eggplant suit. But I got to tell you, Pru, I'm not partial to eggplants or you in suits. Eggplant tastes like fried sponge, and you in suits is not what I like. Fact is, I like you in nothing at all.'' He ducked when she threw the next pillow, then continued. ''So, I got you something else, instead. Something that reminds me of you when you're out here on the ranch.'' He brought his hands from behind his back and tossed a black Stetson onto the middle of the bed. ''You're not a city girl anymore, that's for sure. You're a cowgirl, a damn fine cowgirl who's taken on a lot of work out here. A cowgirl needs a hat.''

She planted her hands on her hips, looking from the hat to Brice. ''How exactly do you mean 'cowgirl'?''

Brice pushed his own hat to the back of his head and folded his arms across his chest. He gave her a cocky smile. ''Well, the girl part I know about from firsthand experience.'' His left eyebrow arched in a suggestive manner. ''And likewise for the cow part.''

A grin crept across her own face, then she laughed because she couldn't hold it in. ''I'm not sure if that's a compliment or not, but I love the hat.'' She snatched it from the middle of the bed. ''Oh, look, it has a row of little silver cows for the band. Isn't that cute.''

''Stetsons are not 'cute.'''

She unpinned her hair and put on the hat, cinching it down tight on her head. ''There.'' She turned in a circle to be admired.

''Not like that. You're wearing it like some city-slicker.''

He came into the room and took the hat off her head. ''Let me tell you about this particular hat. First off, consider the color—it's black, in case you want to go for another mud ride with my cows. It'll hide the dirt a lot better than your suit did.'' He ran his finger down the middle. ''See here—it has a single deep crease. That makes it good for water drainage, in case you get another hankering to go back on the roof in a rainstorm.''

''You're enjoying this, aren't you.''

His eyes danced. ''You made fun of the sleeping bags. It's my turn.''

''Then, I guess it's my turn again.'' She pushed him backward. He stumbled, then fell onto the bed, spread-eagle across the yellow bedspread. She picked the pillow from the floor, ready to pummel him again, but instead dropped it back to the floor. She took her Stetson from Brice's hand, put it on her head, then slowly unbuttoned her blouse. ''What say we christen this new bed?''

His eyes widened.

''Then we should go downstairs and christen that new couch.''

His eyes went as dark as Godiva chocolates. Hmm, is that why she craved chocolate so much?

''Then what should we do?'' he asked.

''Then, cowboy, I go out and order us more furniture.''

Chapter Nine

Prudence felt Brice's leg wrapped over hers and his arm draped over her shoulder. Sun streamed through the bedroom window, turning the new yellow comforter golden. His right hand cupped her left breast, and his slow, even breathing warmed the back of her neck. She was in heaven. Or as close to heaven as one got in this world. Brice was an incredible lover. Not that she had much to compare him to, but the way he made her feel was simply not of this planet.

She rolled over to face him. His arms trapped her in an embrace, and he smiled. She said, "I take it you're not sleeping."

"I can sleep later. With you here, I can think of much better things to do." His fingers trailed up her spine and tangled in her hair.

"Dad came to see me this afternoon."

His fingers stilled, and his eyes snapped open. "Uh-oh."

"You just had to go poking around in stuff that was none of your business?"

"It seemed like a good idea at the time."

"Oh, really."

"Well, he doesn't give you enough credit for being...smart, capable and resourceful. You're incredibly resourceful, you know. You have a lot of good ideas, and even help me with—" He stopped and raised his eyebrows. "You're baiting me along here, aren't you?"

"Yeah, it's great. You don't have to stop."

"Well, now that you mention it, you do make the best fried chicken in all of Serenity, but you must swear not to tell Aunt Lilly I said that, or she'll skin me alive."

Pru made a cross over her heart in pledge. "For your information, things between Dad and me are better than ever. So thanks for the cooking compliment and thanks for interfering." She kissed him on the cheek. "But you should know, this gives me license to interfere in your life when I get the chance."

His hand dropped to the small of her back, and he pressed her body tightly to his. The laughter in his eyes died, giving way to the heated look of passion. His desire for her pressed hard against her leg. "Want to do a little interfering right now?" He kissed her, then covered her body with his.

An hour later, Brice cuddled Pru in his arms and watched her sleep. He thought of how they'd just made love. This time had been slow, agonizingly so, neatly driving him out of his mind with wanting. And it had been delicious since he'd tasted her hair, her lips, her throat, the soft flesh of her belly, the sweetness of her desire for him. It had been incredibly sensuous as he felt her shudder and quiver with passion. He'd never tire of holding her like this, of being with her in and out of bed, of talking with her and making plans with her. The problem was, would his family—and hers—be a constant wedge between them? More important, could he and Pru ever get beyond that if this idea to end the feud didn't pan out?

The phone in the kitchen rang, and Pru muttered, "Let it ring. Your cows can wait and the oil's been in the ground for centuries. A few more hours can't matter."

"What if it's the bank? What if there's a tax question? What if you miss out on buying a choice piece of property in town?"

Pru wrinkled her nose. "Drat!"

Cursing the fact that there was no phone extension in the bedroom, Brice slid out from between the warm sheets, then ran barefoot—and bare everything else—to the kitchen, catching the phone on the fifth ring.

By the time he finally hung up the phone, a part of him wished he hadn't answered it. He had turned to go back upstairs, when he spotted Pru in the doorway of the kitchen. She was wearing his shirt, which revealed more than a hint of cleavage and only covered her to mid-thigh. Her hair was mussed from their lovemaking, and her lips were round and full from his kisses. The new couch was only a few steps away, just begging to be christened.

She said, "You've got that 'something's wrong' look on your face. What's up?"

He sighed, tearing his thoughts away from making love to Pru. "It's the south range. Some of the fences are down and cattle are missing. It could be just one of those things, or it could be rustlers. Every spring this happens. Rustlers have worked the area in the past, but there's no way of knowing if it's that, or just fence needing mending, until we scout around. Uncle Judd and his boys are up there now rounding up strays, but I should go take a look, too."

"Can't Judd and his boys handle it?"

"Pru—"

"I know, I know, *you* run the Half-Circle." She let out a deep breath. "Did you ever stop to think that maybe the Half-Circle runs you?"

"As much as Randolph Inc. runs you?"

She raked her hair with her hand, sending auburn strands flying and his hormones on a rampage. "So, what are we going to do about Pine Tree Ridge? Postpone it?"

"I'll be back in two days. Promise."

"Two days." She sighed in resignation. "Well, that will give me time to get some work done at the bank for a change. Maybe I can even clean out the rest of the closets for the Garden Society sale and drop off those letters to Grandma Eulah."

"You'll be busier than me. Say, when you're in town, could you remind Hoof and Hardware to deliver the materials to the ridge on Saturday? I'll have Derek come over and feed the cattle, and let him spring our plan on the rest of the McCormacks. Probably better coming from him, anyway. It won't look so contrived. He'll undoubtedly try to rustle the down payment on a new truck out of me for all this—but he'll do it."

He went to her and tipped her chin, bringing her face close to his. "This idea of ours is going to work, Pru. It has to. I'll meet you at the ridge on Sunday at noon, if I have to ride one of my own cows to get there. Keep the faith, okay, darlin'?"

She gave him a wide-eyed look and bit back a laugh. "Darlin'? Where'd that come from?"

"Well, now, that's cowboy talk for when the menfolk—that's me—have to leave their womenfolk—that's you—behind and head on out to the range." He brushed his lips across hers. "It gets lonesome out on that range, darlin'."

And that was true. He knew all about loneliness because he'd been alone most of his adult life, on and off the range, sharing very little of his thoughts and problems with anyone. Until now.

PRUDENCE STOOD TIPTOE on the top of a stack of books and reached the top shelf of the bedroom closet. Sunny said, "You're going to kill yourself using those books as a ladder, and with all that's going on at Pine Tree Ridge Sunday, you can't afford to be dead."

Prudence grunted as she reached a little farther. "There's something back there, I can feel it."

Sunny rolled up her shirtsleeves and tugged a carton of books across the hardwood floor and into the hallway. ''Let it go—we've got enough stuff for the Buttons and Bows Sale.''

''Ross Restorations said I should get anything I want out of the closets before they start enlarging them next week. I can still feel one more bundle of something way in the back. It might be another pack of Grandma Eulah's letters. I know she'd like to have them. Thought I'd surprise her with them tomorrow. We can all do lunch. My treat.''

Sunny did a backward shuffle, dragging the box as she went. ''If we end up doing lunch in the hospital while you're in traction, that is not going to be a treat, and Brice will have my head for putting his new wife out of commission, if you know what I mean.''

''What I need is more books to stand on,'' Prudence said as she stepped off her perch.

Sunny stood and propped her hands on her hips. ''Do you ever listen to anyone?''

''Depends if I like what they're saying.'' Prudence flashed a devilish grin as she added another handful of books to her stack. ''There. That should be enough.''

''Enough to get yourself killed.'' Sunny slid the box the rest of the way into the hall.

Prudence gingerly stepped onto the wobbly stack. ''It's perfect.''

Sunny reappeared in the doorway and said, ''A perfect accident waiting to happen, if you're asking me. Don't do anything until I get over there to hold on to you.''

''No need.'' Prudence reached into the closet and easily nabbed the parcel. ''Got it.'' She inched the parcel forward. ''Piece of cake.'' She stretched again to get a better hold, and felt the books begin to tip. ''Sunny?'' Prudence grabbed the shelf as the books under her slid sideways.

''Prudence!'' Sunny raced across the room to grab Prudence, but missed as Prudence toppled onto the floor, taking the shelf and bundle of papers with her.

Sunny knelt down next to Prudence. ''My stars, girl. Are you all right? Say something.''

''Ouch!''

''Prudence, dear heart, I'm thinking as long as you're living out here you should consider upping your medical insurance a tad. Are you all right or not?''

''I'm...just...peachy.'' Her voice sounded like a puffy squeak; the wind had been knocked clean out of her lungs.

''Should I call 911?''

Prudence shook her head. ''Just give me a minute to see if all my parts still work.''

Sunny picked up one of the papers that had fallen from the shelf, while Prudence made sure she could move her fingers and toes. Sunny said, ''You'll be unhappy to know you just risked your neck for an electric bill from 1972.''

Sunny fanned through the rest to the stack of papers. ''In fact, this bundle you were trying to reach is bills from 1972.'' Sunny slid another paper from the stack. ''Look here, the Dillards bought a refrigerator for two hundred dollars. Now, those were the good old days.'' She picked up a few more bills. ''Don't think Eulah has any interest in old bills.''

Pru sat up and took a deep breath, feeling good that this time the air went all the way down her windpipe. She shook her head to clear her thoughts. ''At least I have that one bundle of letters for her. She'll like that.'' As Prudence studied the scattered books on the floor, her gaze suddenly landed on a splotch of faded yellow. ''What's this?'' she asked as she picked up a dried flower petal from the floor.

Sunny bent toward Prudence and looked closer. ''Well, now, I'd say it's a rose petal. Looks like a yellow Peace Rose, if you ask me, and there are more petals over by that shelf that crashed on the floor right along with you.''

''Let's not talk about anything crashing on the floor right now, okay?'' Prudence said as she reached for the shelf and picked up one end. There were faded letters of some kind lying on the floor with the rest of the yellow rose. The yellow rose had a bow tied around the stem, with Eulah's name on a discolored, heart-shaped card.

''Oh, my gosh. Sunny, these must be love letters from Granddad Thomas the year before he and Eulah married. This is such a great find. Eulah must have tacked them under that old shelf the summer she stayed with the Dillards, then forgotten about them.''

Prudence felt her face light up with happiness. "She'll love getting these."

"Look again, dear."

"Look at what?"

"Look at the bottom of the letter that's over by your knee. The one that's half open, with the bottom part showing. It's signed 'All my love, Wes.'" Sunny looked Prudence dead in the eye. "Wes is not Thomas."

"Letmeseethat." Prudence snatched the letter from the floor and stared at the signature. Her heartbeat rocketed, her head seemed to be floating off her shoulders. What was going on here?

Sunny said, "We shouldn't be snooping. No good has ever come from snooping, I can tell you that, and if you unfold the rest of that there letter, you'll be snooping like all get-out."

Prudence could barely breathe. "What if this letter is to Eulah?"

"It's none of our business, Prudence."

"What if Eulah and Wes were…were…involved?" Prudence swallowed. "Lovers, maybe?"

"It's none of our business, Prudence."

"Eulah and Wes have put me and Brice through a living hell for years with their constant arguing and battling. Do you know how many times Brice and I have gone to court because of these two doing battle? How could they do that? How could they pretend to be enemies all these years when…when… I have a right to know, Sunny. Blast them."

Prudence whipped open the letter, and immediately wished she hadn't.

"What?" Sunny asked. "What is it? You look like death warmed over."

Prudence handed the letter to Sunny. "Seventy years ago, Cilus McCormack knew there was oil on the Half-Circle before he bought out Jacob Randolph's share. Wes told Eulah because they were trying to put an end to the feud even then, and he thought this might force a compromise between the families."

Prudence faced Sunny. "What am I going to do? If I give this letter to my dad, he'll go after the Half-Circle like a duck on a June bug. He's just looking for an excuse to do that—he has been all his life." Prudence felt her heart thud. "Brice could lose a huge portion of his land."

"But, Prudence dear, blood is blood. You are a Randolph, the next head of the Randolph family. Is it fair to the Randolphs to have been tricked out of what was rightfully theirs? You can't just pretend this letter doesn't exist, though...if you hadn't read it like I suggested you—"

"I know, I know." Prudence closed her eyes and prayed the earth would swallow her up. When that didn't happen, she looked at Sunny and continued. "But I did read the letter. What am I going to do about it? I have to choose between my family and Brice."

"Prudence, dear, could you really live with yourself if you didn't tell your father and the rest of the family? This is something that has to be settled by both families, not just you. It's not your decision to make.''

Prudence felt her heart crack. She was sure it did, because no other pain could be so harsh. ''Brice will hate me for the rest of his life. How am I going to tell him I'm the one responsible for putting the Half-Circle in jeopardy?''

IT WAS ALMOST ELEVEN when Brice turned onto the gravel road that lead to Pine Tree Ridge. The two days he'd just spent with his uncle and cousins had to have been the longest days in history. Even the fact that the sky today was Texas-blue and a gentle breeze was whistling through the pines didn't put him in a good mood.

How could anything compensate for sleeping on hard ground instead of wrapped in Pru's arms, smelling bovine instead of warm vanilla, listening to cowboy talk and banter instead of Pru's conversation and easy laughter? He was a bit early for the meeting of the families, and he prayed Pru was early, too. If he didn't get at least one kiss from her before everyone showed up to work this afternoon, he'd be ornery as an overpacked mule for the rest of the day.

Making the last turn to the top of the ridge that marked the picnic area, Brice heard the distant thud of hammers at the same time as he caught sight of trucks and various older SUVs parked everywhere. There were two pickups with the Half-Circle brand painted on the side, and other trucks he knew belonged to his younger relatives.

A few souped-up classic sports cars were parked side-by-side, and some compacts were lined up beside Pru's Lincoln. Farther up the hill, he saw the younger set of McCormacks and Randolphs hauling lumber.

Damn. So much for being early. He and Pru wouldn't get two seconds alone, now. He should have let Uncle Judd and his boys finish mending the fences without him. He should have come home earlier. Maybe he should have let Judd handle the whole broken fence thing and not have left Pru in the first place.

He'd never before felt that way about running the Half-Circle. It was unsettling. The ranch was his world—except that he had Pru in his life now, and that made a difference.

Brice spotted her standing among boxes of nails, shingles and piles of two-by-fours and four-by-fours. Off to one side was a table crowded with covered dishes and pots. Wooden half-barrels nearby probably held drinks. Once again, Pru had outdone herself, taking charge of the situation when he wasn't around.

She was wearing her cowgirl hat and one of his flannel shirts that fit her like a coat. It was…familiar, intimate. His insides stirred, remembering when they had last made love, and she'd worn that hat and nothing else. She looked incredibly sexy—though, Pru could be wearing a grain sack and goulashes right now, and he'd undoubtedly think that was sexy, too.

He'd missed her more than he'd ever have thought possible! Every inch of him wanted her right this very minute, and with a little encouragement from her he'd be willing to find a deserted patch of grass, or hillside or even the back seat of her Lincoln, and show her just how *much* he'd missed her.

Derek rapped on the door of Brice's truck, making him jump in his seat and yanking his thoughts to what was happening around him. He said to Derek, "Isn't everyone here a little...early? Thought I said noon. It's ten, that's not noon." He resisted the urge to growl out the last sentence.

Derek pushed his Stetson back on his head. "Well, now, there you go getting all picky. It just so happens that some of the more reasonable cousins and me got to talking and thought it'd be a mighty good idea for us to meet early to set things up here. Then I kind of let Sally Randolph know what we planned, and lo and behold if she and some of her more reasonable cousins didn't come early, too." Derek assumed a young-stud kind of look. "Worked out real nice, if ya ask me."

"How long have you all been working?"

Derek checked his watch. "One hour and fifteen minutes, and no one's had a fight yet. I'd say fighting is the last thing on their minds. It's nice not to have to sneak around and pretend we don't want anything to do with each other, when we really do. Usually we just have to accidentally show up at the same place. But today we're *supposed* to be here."

For a moment Brice remembered when he'd been

in that situation. Pru had always fascinated the hell out of him. He could still remember going to Sundae Annie's Ice Cream Parlor just to see Pru. 'Course, she was a Randolph, and seeing was all he could do.

Brice asked, ''Think Granddad Wes, Uncle Judd and the rest will show?''

''Oh, they'll come because they're curious about you and Prudence, if nothing else. Everybody's going to be here.'' Derek looked around, catching Sally Randolph's eye as she strutted around carrying a hammer that she obviously had no intention of using. She was a cute girl—Randolph-cute with auburn hair and blue eyes. Not as cute as Pru, of course, but then no one was as cute as his Pru. Hmm, he liked the sound of that. He wanted Pru to be ''his'' for a long, long time.

Derek said, ''You know, big brother, now that we're here, I think this idea of yours was a pretty darn good one. Your marrying Prudence was even better. Sort of paves the way for the rest of us.'' He hitched his chin toward Sally and said to Brice, ''I owe you.''

''Owe me enough to forfeit the down payment on that new truck you want?''

Derek looked at Brice and howled with laughter. Then he headed back to the building site, where he snagged Sally around the waist, and they headed for the woods. At this rate the shelter wouldn't get finished until the next millennium, thought Brice. But the McCormacks and Randolphs were getting along, hallelujah for that.

Brice parked the truck, then headed toward Pru. She hadn't noticed him yet; she was busy pointing out lumber, handing out bags of nails and showing the way to food and drinks. In a momentary lull, he came up behind her, whisked off her hat and planted a kiss on the side of her neck.

"Brice?" She dropped the bucket of nails she'd been holding and gasped.

He took another little taste of her sweetness. "It damn well better be Brice," he said on a laugh. He turned her around and grinned as he settled her hat back on her head. "Miss me?"

Pru's eyes were shadowed as if she hadn't slept, and her mouth was too serious. He said, "Lighten up, cowgirl. Everything's going to be all right. It looks like these kids are interested in having fun more than fighting, and that's closer than our families have been in years." He kissed her warm lips, and felt desire shoot through him like a bolt of prairie lightning. Every time he kissed her, something incredible happened.

"We...we have an audience, you know." She mouthed the words next to his lips. She was wound tighter than an eight-day clock.

"We're married, remember?"

Her gaze connected with his. Her eyes were anxious as she said, "I remember very well. Very, very well, and I want you to remember that, too." She let out a deep sigh, gave him a quick kiss, then bent down and started picking up the nails.

This was all having a bad effect on her. He

couldn't remember ever having seen her quite so upset. Pru was acting downright twitchy. He looked at his watch. Well, in seven hours it would all be over with a happy ending, and Pru would be back to her old self again. Then he could get her all to himself. Trouble was, seven hours was a hell of a long time to wait. He bent down and helped her pick up the nails.

"How are things going so far?"

"So far?"

"With the kids? Are you okay?"

"With this group it's a case of hormones winning out over feuding."

"This I can definitely relate to." He shared a grin with Pru as they stood, but her expression seemed forced. He took the nails and set the pail on a stack of wood. He placed his hands on her shoulders and studied her closely. "What's wrong, Pru? I've never seen you like this."

Granddad Wes's red pickup suddenly skidded around the corner, throwing loose gravel and mud everywhere. One look at that truck, and Brice knew Granddad was in a bad mood. He said, "I'm going to try to settle Wes down before he starts making problems where there aren't any. You watch out for your dad and Grandma Eulah, and see if you can do the same when they get here. If we get them to coexist for today, half the battle's won." Brice kissed Pru, then gave her a lopsided grin. "That's for luck. And don't be so worried. It's going to work, Pru. I know it."

Then he took off toward the red truck. "Granddad," Brice yelled, as Wes got out. "Mighty happy to see you here. Glad you could make it. We can use your help."

Wes yanked the brim of his ten-gallon hat down hard on his forehead and scrutinized the area. "Whose dang-fool idea was it to get Randolphs up here working on building something? The only thing they can build is trouble. Bet this idea belonged to that gal you married."

Brice bristled but decided this was a time to smooth feathers instead of ruffle them. "Granddad, that gal is my wife, and it was *her* idea to get Randolphs and *mine* to get the McCormacks involved. Everyone uses this area, and we can work together to fix it up for the town. That's not asking too much."

"Depends who you're asking." Wes heaved his toolbox from the bed of his pickup.

Brice draped his arm over his grandfather's shoulder. "Come on over and have some fried chicken and potato salad, before you get to work. I think Pru cooked for days to get this all together."

"Don't want no Randolph fried chicken. Who knows what's in it?"

Brice nodded to the younger set. "They've been chowing down for the past hour and don't look any the worse for it."

"Humph, what's your uncle Judd going to think if he sees me gnawing on Randolph chicken?"

"Probably that he wished he had a piece or two himself." Brice headed Granddad toward the food table. ''How about a long-neck to cool you off, then you can decide about eating.''

''Nope. Came here to work and that's what I'm aiming to do. Besides, we can't have the Randolphs soaking up all the glory for taking care of Serenity. This here is a McCormack town, too. Think I'll go help those young people up the hill a ways. Don't look like they got any notion about what they're doing, except fooling around.''

''What about working on some picnic tables?'' Brice encouraged, hoping to give the young people a little more time together. ''No one's working on those.''

''Making picnic tables is for some namby-pamby city person who doesn't know which end of the hammer to use. Save that for the Randolphs.''

Brice saw three of his uncles get out of their trucks and follow Wes. Then he looked back to the food table and saw Pru talking to her dad.

The sight of Bob Randolph dressed in jeans and flannel shirt was unnerving as hell. For as long as Brice could remember, he'd only seen Pru's dad in expensive suits and ties. Pru and her father were lost in some serious discussion that Pru didn't seem too happy about. She looked completely stressed, far more so than when Brice had left her two days ago. He should never have gone to the south pasture.

For the moment, the only loud sounds were hammering and sawing. No yelling, no threatening, no fighting. Already things were off to a better start than the wedding.

''Yoo-hoo,'' Sunny called from a blue truck as it

pulled into the parking area. ''Prudence, Brice, we're here.'' Her truck and four others stopped behind the Willises', and Sunny called again as she got out, ''The Serenity Garden Society's all ready to get to work.''

Sunny, the judge and a small parade of McCormack, Randolph and impartial men and woman began collecting flats of daisies, buttercups, day lilies and small trees from the backs of trucks and Jeeps.

Pru waved, but was looking worse by the minute. He had to get her to sit down and relax. After all, everything was going well.

''Who would have thought that it was possi—'' Brice swallowed his last syllable as he spotted Derek in a flat-out run, coming up the drive. His brother's face was pinched with concern, and he was breathing hard by the time he reached Brice, who asked, ''Now what?''

''A car wreck. Uncle Judd and Ms. Eulah ran into each other when they both tried to turn into the drive at the same time.''

''How bad?''

''Just bad enough to cause trouble.''

Brice ground his boot into the ground. ''Sounds like we're back to business as usual. Is everyone yelling and screaming insults and arguing over insurance?''

''Yeah, but there's more.'' Derek exhaled a deep, exasperated breath and looked Brice in the eyes. ''You and I both know the feud's had its share of cussing and swearing, split lips, black eyes and bruises. This time things have gotten out of hand. I think Eulah's arm is broken.''

PRUDENCE COULD TELL by the serious look on Derek's usually happy face that something was wrong, even more wrong than usual when McCormacks and Randolphs got together. And that, in addition to those blasted letters from Wes to Eulah, was sure to head both families into a worse feud rather than the one that already existed. How was she going to tell Brice?

And she had to do it soon, because she'd already given the letters to her father.

''What happened?'' she asked Brice.

He took a deep breath, then said, ''It's your grandmother. There was an accident at the bottom of the hill and Eulah's arm might be broken—''

Prudence didn't wait to hear another word. She took off for the drive. As if alerted by some inborn family radar system, she knew other Randolphs were following right behind her—and probably McCormacks right along with them.

When Prudence rounded the last turn she heard arguing and swearing and saw the side of Judd McCormack's truck mashed to the side of Grandma Eulah's white Lincoln. The driver's side of the Lincoln was open, and Sally was hunkered down beside Eulah. Prudence joined her.

''Grandma, how bad is your arm?''

''Well, I suppose I'm going to survive, but no thanks to the McCormacks, as usual.''

Bob Randolph stuck his head in the Lincoln. ''Eulah? What happened?''

''That no-account cowboy, Judd McCormack, and his hee-haw car ran me plumb off the road,'' Eulah yelled, loud enough for the gathering crowd to hear.

Judd pushed his gray Stetson to the back of his head and said, ''Like hell I did. I didn't run you anywhere, Eulah. You cut me off when I came around the bend and tried to pass you! This here wreck's all your fault. Where'd you learn to drive, anyway?''

Eulah wormed her way out of the car and stood, holding her arm. Her face was red and her eyes beady. She shot back with ''Why would you try to pass me, you low-down varmint? You can't pass on this here road, everybody knows that.''

''I can if you're only doing five miles an hour, you old bat. You turned right into me when I went around you. Look what you've done to my car.''

''Look what you've done to my arm.''

Brice made his way to the front of the crowd, and stood between Eulah and Judd. ''Everybody just be quiet.''

Bob Randolph retorted, ''Who are you telling to be quiet?''

Granddad Wes glared. ''Brice is, because you and Eulah are making so dern much noise, no one can even think straight.''

Bob faced Granddad Wes. ''From what I've seen, McCormacks never could think straight about nothing. They sure as heck don't know how to drive a nail right or how to hammer two boards together, for that matter. Never seen such shameful work as what you do, Wes.''

''Now just a goldarn minute,'' Wes replied. ''No city-slicker lawyer's going to be telling me how to build anything. McCormacks have been building for many a year now.''

''Yeah,'' Bob Randolph snarled. ''They sure enough have. And they've been doing that building on Randolph land for the past seventy years.''

''Says you,'' roared Granddad Wes.

''Yeah, says me,'' yelled Bob Randolph. ''And now I've got the proof to back up the Randolph claim.''

A long, loud horn blast drew everyone's attention to the truck making its way down the drive. Derek maneuvered his pickup around the crowd and the wrecked cars. He pulled to a stop and got out. ''Prudence, you can use my truck to take your grandmother to the hospital.''

Eulah squared her shoulders and raised her chin. ''I'm not riding in any McCormack truck. You can bet your bottom dollar on that.''

Prudence felt her self-control snap. ''Grandmother, for crying out loud, get in the truck. You're going to the hospital, I'm going to take you there, and you're going to thank Derek McCormack for being kind enough to offer his truck for transportation.''

''When pigs fly! I'd just as soon walk to the hospital.'' And she headed down the road.

Chapter Ten

As Prudence turned her Lincoln down the new gravel lane that lead to the ranch house, she watched the last rays of sunset dip behind the rolling hills, turning pinks, purples and blues to shades of navy and gray. How could a day filled with so many problems end in such a beautiful array of colors? And her problems weren't over yet. There was still the letter debacle to deal with.

Her stomach ached at the thought. How was she going to tell Brice what she'd done? How could she have done otherwise? She parked her car next to his truck and trudged toward the house. Halfway there she spotted Brice sitting on the front steps—the new front steps of her house.

''How's Eulah?'' he asked.

''After I caught up with her a half-mile down the road and persuaded her to get her fanny in my car even though I'm married to a McCormack, she was okay. Her wrist isn't broken, no thanks to Judd. How could he run an old woman off the road?''

Brice leaned forward, resting his forearms on his

thighs. He gave Prudence a long, hard look. "If you want my opinion, it looked more like Eulah turned in to him, trying to keep him from passing her. The cars scraped against each other more than hit."

"My grandmother was hurt, Brice. Her wrist was sprained."

"Knowing Eulah, it was from giving my uncle some creative hand sign when he tried to drive around her. She was probably hogging the road like she always does and going five miles an hour just to tick him off." He heaved a deep sigh, still looking at the ground and not at Prudence. "Our great plan didn't work out too great. Not only are our families battling worse than ever, but now we are, too." He patted a space next to him on the step. "Sit down. We can work this out."

"Maybe."

He slowly brought his gaze to hers. He looked so tired and drained, and now she was going to break his heart and probably hers, too. In five minutes all their plans and dreams would go right down the toilet, and it was her fault. Why had she given those papers to her dad? Then again, as head of the Randolph family, how could she not? The bottom line on all this was that the McCormacks had swindled the Randolphs. Period.

"Pru, Eulah is going to be—"

"This isn't about Eulah." Her stomach churned. She had to sit down, but that was the coward's way out. No, she'd made her decision when she handed over the letter; now she had to tell Brice what she'd done. "Actually, it is about Eulah, sort of, but not about the accident. It's about the feud."

"Pru, everything's about the feud."

"You know the letters I found, the ones belonging to Eulah. I found a few more. They were from Wes."

If the situation hadn't been so dire, she would have laughed at the dumbfounded look on Brice's face. She continued, "It seems they were once sweethearts."

"Sweet...Sweet...?"

"They exchanged letters, confidences—they wanted to end the feud. And in one of the letters Wes confessed that his granddaddy had told him that the McCormacks did, in fact, know about the oil before buying out the Randolphs."

Brice shot to his feet. Disbelief over what she'd said mixed with anger, and he stared right at her. What had she expected? Diamonds and roses?

"I want to see this letter," he demanded.

"I gave it to my dad."

His anger escalated; she could see it in his eyes. Then betrayal and hurt followed. She could barely breathe from the pain in her heart. Tears stung her eyes. But she refused to cry. She was the one who'd put this look on Brice's face, and she'd have to live with it.

He said, "If these letters are authentic, why didn't Eulah bring them out herself years ago?"

"They are real letters, Brice. I asked Eulah about them, and she didn't deny anything, but she didn't volunteer anything else."

''What does Bob intend to do?''

Prudence shook her head. ''I don't know.''

''How could you do this? *Why* did you do this, Pru?''

''I'm a Randolph. What was I supposed to do, Brice? Ignore the whole thing? Pretend I didn't see the letters?''

''For starters, you could have waited till I came home. We could have discussed it.''

''So I could hand the letters over to you? This is probably going to wind up in court, and the way I see it, that's a good thing. It will put an end to the feud once and for all.''

''And an end to the Half-Circle.''

''If Cilus McCormack had been straightforward from the get-go, this all could have been avoided. Besides, I think there's something else going on with Eulah and Wes. They were trying to end the feud and be together. But it didn't work out for them.''

''And it's not working out for us.''

She felt weak. ''I'm going to fix dinner. We'll eat and figure out what to do next.''

''We? After this, there is no 'we.' You made your choice and it's the Randolphs. I think you should go home.''

Even though she'd suspected he'd say something like that, his words stabbed right through her. ''I am home. We're married, Brice, so technically this house is still my home. And to tell you the truth, arguing with you is a whole lot easier than listening to my family explaining to me in great detail just how awful the McCormacks are. I know better. I've heard enough McCormack-bashing to last me forever."

"If you don't leave, Pru, I will."

"This is your land, and you have to take care of the cattle. And maybe, if you and I can present a united front, showing we can work things out, our families will come to some compromise, too."

"There is no compromise when it comes to the Half-Circle. It belongs to the McCormacks. We've worked it and made it what it is today." His eyes were cold when he looked at her. "You betrayed me, Pru."

"And if I hadn't turned over those letters, I would have betrayed my family. Tell me, Brice, what would you do if you were in my shoes?"

He looked at her for a moment, then turned and headed for the barn. She went inside the house, closing the new oak-and-glass door behind her, leaning against it for a moment, trying to forget about the day and let the smell of fresh paint and varnish wash over her. The only things she knew for sure were that she was staying here and that she was sleeping on the couch. She couldn't sleep in the brass bed upstairs, where she and Brice had made love, but she was *not* leaving her house.

Why had she read that letter? Sunny had warned her that snooping led to no good, and the woman had been so very right. Maybe she shouldn't have given the letter to her dad. Then again, could she live with herself if she didn't? There had to be some way for the Randolphs to get what was rightfully theirs and for the Half-Circle to stay with the McCormacks. But she had no clue what that way could possibly be.

She sat down on the couch and gazed out the window, watching daylight fade to night. She laid her head back, closed her eyes and slept...only to be awakened by a terrible pounding on the front door.

Her eyes shot open and her stomach rolled. She had no idea how long she'd been asleep, but the house was now dark.

More knocking echoed through the house, making her head throb. "I'm coming, I'm coming." She fumbled around for the floor lamp and finally managed to turn it on. Her stomach lurched as she made her way to the front door and looked out the side window. Whoever it was, they were so close to the door she couldn't see them. "Who's there?"

"Pru?"

Brice? It didn't sound like him. It didn't sound like anyone she knew.

She looked out the peephole in the door but couldn't see a thing. If she stayed out here on the ranch, she was going to get a dog. Something with a lot of teeth. She grabbed a can of varnish from the floor. If she was desperate, she could throw it at the person on the other side. When he doubled up with laughter, she could make her getaway.

Cautiously, she opened the door—to find Brice standing on the porch. Actually, he was supporting himself in the doorway with one hand on one side of the door frame and one on the other. His shirt was torn, his eye swollen, his jaw bruised, his lip split, his hat backward.

"What happened to you?"

"I had a little altercation in town."

"Let me guess, with a Randolph."

"Every dang one of them I could find, darlin'." He stumbled, and she caught him before he fell, letting most of his weight land on her.

She put the can of varnish back on the floor. "Brice McCormack, you're drunk."

"As a skunk and proud of it."

"Did you drive like this?"

"'Course not. I hitched a ride with good old Sheriff Pritchard. Told me to go sleep it off somewhere. Told him to drop me here 'cause I intend to give you a piece of my mind."

"Right now, you don't have any to spare. Come on in."

"I don't want any part of a Randolph house that—"

"Brice. Just shut up. I want you to walk over to the couch. I'll help you."

"Don't want your help."

"Tough." She shuffled him into the house and onto the couch. "I'm going to get some water and aspirin and ice. Just lie down. And don't you dare throw up on our new couch."

As she went into the kitchen, she reasoned that this was all her fault. Brice had never behaved like this in his whole life. Probably because no one had ever seriously threatened to take the Half-Circle away from him. And the Half-Circle was his, totally and completely. If she could undo one thing in her life, it would be reading that damn letter.

When she went back into the living room, Brice was sprawled across the couch. It had seemed really big...until now. "Wake up." She knelt down beside him.

"Uh-uh."

She poured two aspirin into her hand, then cradled Brice's head. "Open your mouth and take these." She held the glass for him and encouraged him to drink. Then she put ice wrapped in a towel on his lip and one on his head, and watched him drop back to sleep.

She loved him. She loved him with every bone in her body. She'd known that for some time, now, but was afraid to admit it because things just might not work out.

Well, guess what, skippy? Things didn't work out any worse than this, and she loved him now more than ever. Nothing between Randolphs and McCormacks followed a logical path—why should her love for Brice be any different? And whatever happened between their families, it wouldn't alter her feelings for Brice one iota. She digested that for a moment.

Suddenly she heard the crunch of a car on gravel. Someone else was coming? This wasn't the old Dillard ranch, it was Serenity's answer to Grand Central Station. The car lights died, and a moment later she heard footsteps on the porch. Looking out the peephole, this time she saw Judge Willis. She opened the door, and the judge nearly fell into the room, his hand raised mid-knock.

She asked, "What happened now?"

The judge closed the door behind him as he came inside. His hair stood out in all directions, and his clothes had been thrown on without much concern for what went with what. This was not the meticulous Judge Willis who presided in the Serenity courthouse. He ran his hand through his already scary hair and rubbed his graying stubble, while looking from Prudence to Brice.

"We've got a big problem. Your dad phoned me at four a.m.—damn his hide. He wants to meet me at nine sharp at the courthouse. Said he's going to sue the pants off the McCormacks and wants to set up a court date. Figured I should tell you about all this in person, since I got you and Brice—" The judge glanced at Brice on the couch. "What happened to him?"

"Feud overload. Did Sunny tell you about the letter?"

"Yep, and I'm guessing that's what's got your dad on the warpath, and I'm guessing you told Brice and that's why he looks like he lost a fight with a bobcat."

"Well, Judge, what are we going to do now?"

"I don't rightly know. But I want you at the courthouse when your daddy comes through the door. Maybe we can work out a compromise. You never know what's going to happen when things wind up in court, so let's try to avoid that.''

''I'll be there without Brice. If he and my dad get in the same room, all hell will surely break loose. Besides, tomorrow morning my dear husband's not going to be in any shape to go anywhere.''

BRICE PRIED OPEN one heavy eyelid, and immediately shut it when a shaft of sunlight pierced clear through his brain. He had to be the only cowboy in Texas who got drunk on four beers. Never could drink worth a damn. Derek got all the drinking genes. Damn unfair gene pool. Brice touched his other eye that refused to open at all. Ugh. He must have been in a fight. He licked his dry lips and felt the sting of a cut there. Two fights. He flexed his hand, feeling how swollen and sore it was. Damn, he'd been in a whole ton of fights, and this morning he was paying for it.

''Feeling better?'' It was Pru. He gingerly opened his one good eye, careful not to open it too far.

''What am I doing here? I don't want any part of this place or you.''

''Yeah, well, people in hell want ice water, and they don't get that, either. I'm going into town to meet with Willis and my dad to see what he plans to do about the letter.''

''You mean what he plans to do about *my ranch.*'' Brice sat up, feeling worse than when he rode bulls at rodeo time. ''You're not going anywhere without me. It's my ranch you're planning on carving up like a Thanksgiving turkey, and I'm going to do what I can to stop it."

"Suit yourself. We have to leave here in fifteen minutes."

Forty-five minutes later, they pulled into the town square. Brice couldn't believe he had to search for a parking place near the courthouse at eight-thirty in the morning. No wonder he was a rancher; if he had to face this every day, he'd go plumb nuts. He cast a quick glance at Pru. They hadn't talked much since they'd left the ranch, mostly because his stomach and head weren't up to conversation. Besides, what was there to say except "Here we go again."

Pru had on one of her power suits. This one was green, kind of like the skin of a kiwi. He wasn't fond of kiwi, and he hated those suits. They didn't fit the Pru he knew. Then he thought about the letter and decided maybe the suit fit her better than he realized. She was looking bad, really bad, worse than he felt, and that was saying something. "You okay?"

"Jelly belly. That's all. Brice?"

He heaved a big sigh. "I know. You're sorry. But sorry doesn't change much, does it?"

"Actually I was going to tell you that you're parked in a No Parking zone."

He backed out of one space and pulled into another, as Pru said, "Maybe you and Dad can come up with a cash settlement?"

"McCormacks don't have cash like that. The value of the ranch is in the ranch itself and the oil wells." He and Pru sat in the truck for a moment;

neither of them wanted to go into the courthouse. Brice finally said, "For what it's worth, Pru, I thought about what you said, about what I would do if I had found that letter and I was in your shoes." He touched her chin, turning her face toward him. "I honestly don't know what I would do. I guess no one does until they're in that particular place."

Brice slid from behind the wheel, then came around and opened the door for her. Side-by-side they walked toward the courthouse. It wasn't exactly a united front, but they were together when they met up with Bob Randolph coming out the door.

"Prudence, my girl, you're just the person I want to see." Bob had deep circles under his eyes and fatigue lined his face, but his appearance was immaculate as always. He wedged himself between Brice and his daughter, and took Prudence's elbow and ushered her inside the courthouse, heading for Willis's chambers.

Brice followed, grinding his teeth all the way. He wanted to tell Bob Randolph to unhand Pru, that she was his wife and that Bob had no right to come between them. But Bob had already done that to the point where Brice doubted if he and Pru could ever solve their differences. Besides, she was looking sicker by the minute, and another McCormack-Randolph confrontation in City Hall was not what anyone needed right now. He'd settle up with Bob Randolph later.

When they reached Judge Willis's chambers, the judge's secretary showed the three of them in, then closed the door. Brice would bet dollars to a dime that the secretary had her ear pressed firmly to the door at this very moment, and that whatever went on in this room would be top billing on the Serenity gossip circle by nine-thirty at the latest.

"All right," Judge Willis said, after the three of them sat down. "What's this all about, Bob?"

"First off, I hadn't figured on Brice being here, but since it concerns his family, he might as well stay put. I intend to sue the McCormacks for the land their granddaddy swindled out of my granddaddy seventy yeas ago, and I have a fifty-year-old letter written by Wes to Eulah to prove it." Bob waved the letter in the air.

Willis folded his hands on his desk, and his brow furrowed into deep lines. "Bob, why don't you and Brice agree to some kind of out-of-court settlement and set things right once and for all?"

Bob said, "This here's something that should have been done years ago, and I intend to do it now. Half of the McCormack ranch belongs to the Randolphs, and that's just what I aim to prove."

Brice was nearly speechless. Judge Willis looked frazzled. Pru gagged, grabbed the trash can by the judge's desk and threw up.

"Pru?" Brice held her shoulders and rubbed her back. "Are you all right?" He handed her his handkerchief.

Bob huffed. "Of course she's not all right. She's married to a McCormack. What in tarnation could be right about that?"

Pru pulled in a ragged breath. "Dad, that's enough." She took a drink of water from the glass the judge handed her. Brice opened the door to the chamber—nearly toppling the secretary into the room—and handed her the trash can. He figured it was the price she paid for being in the wrong place at the right time.

Brice closed the door, then turned to Bob Randolph and said, "This is getting mighty old, Bob. Letter or no letter, Jacob Randolph got paid for his share of the Half-Circle seventy years ago. You know that, I know that, the whole blamed town knows that. It was a legal transaction. Besides, you can't sue over something that happened way back when. Ever hear of a statute of limitations?"

Bob Randolph glared and waved the letter again. "There was fraud involved—and there are exceptions to every rule, McCormack. I want to take this to court, and then you can kiss part of your ranch goodbye."

Pru looked greener than ever, but stood and faced Bob. "Dad, listen to me. We don't need to go to court. We don't need the Half-Circle Ranch. We have all the money we could ever want. Our family's happy living in town. None of us could saddle a horse if our lives depended on it, and all we know about cows is that we like our steaks medium rare. Why do you want to do this?"

Bob drew himself up proud. "'Bout time a Randolph took what was rightfully his." He looked possessively at Prudence. "You can help me with this. Like I said, it's for the family."

Judge Willis said, "If you're wanting your day in court, Bob, I'm willing to oblige you, just to settle this dang thing. We'll meet in court in two days for an informal hearing to see if a trial's warranted."

Bob nodded. "That's fair enough, Judge." He turned to Prudence. "Come on. We've got a boatload of work to do. Two days doesn't give us much time."

Prudence stood, then turned to her dad and said, "I need to talk to Brice. Alone."

"Why?" Bob asked, sounding aggravated that she'd suggest such a thing.

"Because we're married, and he's my *husband.* Now if you don't mind..."

After her dad and the judge left, Prudence took another sip of water and tried to settle her ailing gut. Brice looked relaxed as a hound dog sleeping by the fire, which meant he wasn't relaxed at all. Prudence paced the room twice, paused in front of the chair where her father had sat, growled, then kicked it over backward.

"I can't believe Dad's doing this."

She watched a lock of black hair dip over Brice's forehead. He was the most handsome man she'd ever met. He was also the most caring, responsible, hard-working person on the planet. And she realized, again, just how much she really did love him—and how close she was to losing him forever.

''I'm not going home with you, Brice. I'm staying in town with Dad.''

''Why am I not surprised?''

''Because you have no faith in the fact that I really want you to keep the Half-Circle.''

''You have a mighty strange way of showing it.''

''You're disappointed and mad as hell that I did this to you. Well, I'm going to try to come up with a way to fix it. I have no idea what that is, but I can't do it from the ranch. I have to see what Dad's up to and talk to Eulah and make some sense of this letter business. There's something we're missing. Something we're not picking up on.''

Brice stood and gave her a hard look. ''Prudence—''

''You never call me that.''

''Well, I am now. Stay wherever it suits you. Do whatever you have to do. But excuse me if I don't put the future of the Half-Circle in your capable Randolph hands. You've already proven where your allegiance lies, and it isn't with me.''

She jabbed her hands on her hips and pulled herself up tall. ''Well, I've got a news flash for you, cowboy. That road runs both ways. When it came to choosing between me or the Half-Circle, we both know what you chose. Your allegiance isn't with me, either. You kicked me to the curb without ever looking back or trying to understand why I did what I did. So don't go blaming me for making the very same decision you did. With us, it is and always will be family first. It doesn't look like anything's going to change that, but I *can* try to see that you keep your ranch fair and square."

"Yeah, right. See you in court."

She watched Brice walk out of the room, then kicked over the chair where he'd been sitting. She eyed both of the upturned chairs. Men! There was never any halfway with them. It was all or nothing, sink or swim, love or hate.

Well, she wasn't a man, and she did believe there was some middle ground somewhere—namely her. She might be the future head of the Randolphs, but she was married to a McCormack. Sounded like middle ground to her. Or was that more like being in the middle and caught in the crossfire? Either way, she was the common factor in this problem, and perhaps Eulah was, too. There had to be some way to pacify the Randolphs and also let the McCormacks keep the ranch.

As far as whether she and Brice would ever get back together, she didn't have a clue. She loved him—but was that enough to overcome all their family problems and the issue of trust and loyalty between the two of them?

THAT AFTERNOON Prudence sat in her office in The First National Bank of Serenity. Her phone was off the hook; one more call about the impending McCormack versus Randolph court case would make her crazy as a woodpecker drumming on a petrified tree.

She ignored the tax work in front of her and gazed

outside, not really seeing anything. Where was Brice right now? What was he doing? Was he feeding the cows that new grain concoction he'd come up with? Did he remember there was leftover fried chicken in the fridge if he got hungry, and his favorite vanilla-bean ice cream in the freezer for dessert?

"Damnation!" She threw a pencil at her office door and barely missed Sunny Willis as she entered. Prudence heaved a weary sigh. "I'm really sorry about that."

Sunny closed the door and sat down in one of the maroon leather chairs across from Prudence's desk. "Rumor has it you've had a rough morning. And for once, I'd say rumor was right."

"I've read about days like this, Sunny. Just never thought it would happen to me. Things keep getting worse and worse. The McCormack and Randolph standoff has deteriorated to an all-time low, and I have no idea how to change it. I've talked myself blue trying to convince Dad this idea to take over Brice's ranch is not only borderline insanity, but morally wrong. I've gotten nowhere. And now I'm stuck in this office, looking out at a two-by-four patch of grass, one skinny tree and a concrete street."

She craned her neck toward the window. "I can't even see the sun from in here. Maybe there isn't any sun, maybe it's just a big electric lightbulb. The only sound is the hum of computers and fax machines." She fiddled with her stapler. "You know, out at the ranch Brice has these great crickets and frogs that make the most awesome sounds. And the cows...did you ever hear cows mooing in the...'' She slowly put the stapler down, then cowered back in her chair. ''I'm clearly losing my mind. What in the name of Aunt Betty's jackass am I going to do about all this?''

''Go back to Brice. It's obvious you're crazy as all get-out about the guy.''

''Right now, that's not counting for much. If I went back to the ranch, he'd probably shoot me for trespassing, since he thinks I sold him down the river...and maybe I did. I should never have read those letters we found.''

''Well, now, hindsight is always twenty-twenty. And could you really have lived with yourself if you hadn't handed the letters over to your dad? You are a Randolph, and that's never going to change, no matter whom you marry. The way I see it, there's got to be a way of settling things. Then you and Brice can find a way to work things out. Did you talk to Eulah again? What puzzles me more than anything is why in tarnation she didn't give that letter to someone long ago.''

''Eulah's lips are closed tighter than a lid on a honey jar.''

''Go see Wes?''

She peered at Sunny as if the woman had clearly lost her mind. ''A little social call at the Half-Circle is not going to get me anywhere except permanent residence in a pine box.''

''Corner him in town. Get him alone. Pressure him.'' Sunny let out a deep sigh. ''The judge feels plumb awful over all this. The poor man's home right now, lying on the couch nursing a killer migraine with a bottle of Jack Daniels."

Prudence stood and paced. "More than one person's taken that approach to our current problem. Maybe I should try it."

"The judge said you lost your breakfast in his trash can."

"Just another high point in my fun-filled day. I have to tell you it's the first time I've lost my breakfast in the judge's chambers, and I've been there more times than I can count."

Sunny folded her hands in front of her and was quiet for a moment before she said, "Uh-oh."

Prudence stopped pacing and turned to Sunny. "Uh-oh, what?"

"Prudence, dear, is there any chance you're the *p* word?"

"Huh?" She considered the question. "Oh, pregnant? Nope. Not a chance. None at all." She shook her head. "I'm positive I'm not. No babies for Brice and me." A twinge crept across her shoulders, and she tried to disregard it. "That would really be the fuse to the dynamite, now, wouldn't it. I mean, McCormacks and Randolphs fight over ranches and who can drive how fast on which roads and who should build what at a park. Just think of what they'd do to a child that belonged to both families."

Sunny took Prudence's hand, before she could start to pace again. This time she looked Prudence right in the eye. "Are you sure? It could be just nerves, but it could be nerves coupled with something else...like a baby on the way."

"I'm positive. In fact, being positive was a high-priority item with us. Once Brice even..." She pictured the condom that Brice had hunted up. The crinkled-up condom in the faded gold package that was a bit dusty and had been buried in the back of Derek's glove compartment under a lot of stuff for heaven knows how long. Did condoms have expiration dates?

"Oh, boy."

"Prudence, I don't want to hear 'oh, boy.' I want to hear more about 'I'm positive.'"

"How about *maybe* I'm positive?"

Sunny let go of Prudence's hand and drummed her fingers on the desktop. "Well, there's only one way to find out for sure if you are or aren't. And if you are, you'll need to make some plans, because that puts a whole new slant on the situation. Like, what in the world are you going to do about this feud and about the father of your baby?"

"Gee, I feel so much better since you put it like that." Prudence crumbled into her chair.

Sunny stood and tucked her purse under her arm as if on a mission. "The first step is to get one of those pregnancy kits at Finn's Drug Store. Think I'll get three to make darn sure. No use worrying if we don't have to."

"I can go."

Sunny went around the desk and hugged Prudence. "Honey child, if you went over there right now, the word would be all over town before you got to the checkout counter.'' She let out a little giggle that made her sound like a young schoolgirl. ''On the other hand, if I go into Finn's and buy pregnancy kits, why, the whole blessed town will think the judge is the Stud of Serenity. It'll do his old ticker good when people start asking questions and making comments about his...manly attributes. It'll get his mind off this here feud, and get everybody talking about something other than the McCormacks and Randolphs for a bit.''

''Glad someone can find something to laugh about in all this.''

Sunny winked. ''I'll be back before you can say 'mommy and daddy.'''

''Not funny,'' Prudence said, as Sunny started out the door. Prudence felt her stomach roll, and she tore for the bathroom. ''Not funny at all,'' she mumbled to herself as she closed the bathroom door behind her.

Chapter Eleven

Brice slammed the door of his truck, kicked a big rock across the yard of the ranch, then tramped out his frustration as he headed toward the house. Work-people were busy scraping the old paint from the side, and, judging by the sounds coming from inside, he suspected there was more work going on there.

The late-morning sun chased the chill from the air and spring buttercups danced in the light breeze. The cloudless sky and a hint of honeysuckle promised another perfect spring day in Texas. But none of that mattered to him one little bit. It wasn't even noon yet, and the day had already been a total disaster.

Halfway to the house, he saw Derek sitting on the top step of the porch. Derek grinned as Brice dropped down next to him, then asked, ''Bad day?''

''Bad as a kick in the butt with a frozen boot.''

''Well, doggies, that *is* bad. What's going on now?''

''Surprised you haven't already heard. The gossips of Serenity have got to be out in full force today.

Telephone company should double their rates, they'd make a killing."

"I've been out of gossip range since last night. Fill me in."

"Were you checking things out on the south pasture like I asked?"

"Talking to Sally Randolph till dawn and taking a walk with her over at Pine Tree Ridge this morning."

Brice paused in his tirade and raised his left eyebrow. "Talking? Walking?"

"That's what I said, and that's what I meant. 'Course, her mama thinks Sally spent the night with her cousin. Now, give me the scoop on what's happening."

"Well, for openers, Bob Randolph is suing us for the Randolph's share of the Half-Circle—whatever the hell that is, I don't know. To top it all off, Pru's the one who gave him a love letter she found from Wes to Eulah that states Cilus knew about the oil—"

"Whoa. Wait a dang minute, here. Wes and Eulah? A...a love letter? I don't believe it."

"Well, you better. And Pru and I have split because of it. I mean, how can I trust her after that? All of which means she isn't here, she's in town and likely to stay there."

"Well, if that don't beat all. Seems to me you two hardheads are at a Mexican standoff. You've chosen your family and ranch over your wife, and she did the same. Trouble is, from the look on your face, I'm guessing you want Prudence back, and I'm guessing she wants you back, too. How do you intend to fix it?''

''Prudence Randolph can stay exactly where she is.''

''Sure she can. Like I said, how do you intend to fix all this?''

''Hell if I know.'' Brice watched a turtle amble across the yard and thought about what Derek had said. Yeah, he wanted Pru back as much as he wanted his ranch. And that was the rub. He couldn't have both. But he missed her, damn it. He missed Pru's cheeky smiles when she one-upped him on something, her soft curls that tumbled in the spring wind, her blue eyes that smoldered when he made love to her, and her pink toenails that tickled him to no end. He missed talking to her about stuff that mattered a lot and stuff that didn't matter diddly. Dang, she belonged sitting here with him, not with anyone else, even if that someone happened to be her father.

But if they got back together, then what? Would she choose him over her family the next time something came up? Would he do the same? Without mutual trust, they had nothing together.

''Guess this long pause in the conversation means either you miss Prudence a powerful lot and don't know what to do about getting her back, or you've fallen asleep with your eyes open.''

Brice shot his brother a withering glance. ''Did you come all the way over here so you'd have an audience for your questionable wit, or did you want to discuss something important?''

''Both. Figured someone of your advanced years can always benefit from my excellent sense of humor.'' Derek reached into his shirt pocket and pulled out a check. He handed it to Brice.

Brice looked at the slip of paper. ''This is the money I gave you for the down payment on your new truck. What's the matter? Not enough?''

Derek shook his head. ''Don't need it. I'll get the truck on my own. Figure if it's all the same to you, I can start taking on more responsibility in running the Half-Circle, now that you've got Prudence on your mind and all. I can earn my own money.''

''You...you want to take on running the Half-Circle?''

''Help out. I'm older than you were when you took on the whole shebang, Brice. 'Bout time I got more involved than just punching cows. I've got a business degree, remember?''

''There's no rush.'' Brice cleared his throat, feeling his world go slightly off-kilter. He had run the ranch for so many years virtually alone, making all the decisions, consulting no one. And now, well, now he didn't know what to do. ''I thought you were trying to impress Sally Randolph. Thought a new truck was just the thing to do that. Sure you don't want to take the check?''

Derek shook his head again. ''Turns out Sally doesn't need impressing.'' A hint of pink followed by crimson inched its way up Derek's neck. ''Truth is, she likes me for who I am. She even likes my jokes.''

''Now, that sounds serious.''

''I'm teaching her how to ride. Bought her a white Stetson. She's teaching me...French.''

Brice nearly fell off the step at that one. ''Little brother, doesn't any of what I'm going through here have an impact on you? You and Sally are going to wind up in the same muddled mess as Pru and me. Pick someone else to teach to ride and buy cowgirl hats for. Concentrate on English. Spare yourself some grief.''

Derek gave Brice a long hard look that suggested he wasn't always the fun-loving guy everyone thought he was. ''Is that how you really feel about Prudence? That you're going to toss her over because she's a Randolph who happened to stumble across some stupid letter?''

''That letter could very well cost us a huge chunk of this ranch.''

''Or not. Your wife is as unhappy with what's going on as you are—I'd bet my boots on that. Never seen a woman look at a man the way Prudence looks at you. She's crazy about you. You think she's fixing this here house up just for herself? I don't think so. Word has it that she's bought brown leather furniture and has bids on several Navajo saddle blankets over in Amarillo. That's not the way Randolphs decorate, that's cowboy stuff. Prudence is furnishing this house with you in mind, brother.''

Before Brice could digest all that, Derek grinned

and continued. ''Guess you should know, Sally and I are waiting till things with you and Prudence settle down to a dull roar, then we're thinking about eloping.''

Brice's gaze connected with Derek's. ''Holy smoke.'' No wonder Derek was pushing for more responsibility. Little brother wasn't so little anymore. But running the Half-Circle? Was Brice ready for anyone to help him do that?

Derek cut into his thoughts with ''Another marriage between a McCormack and a Randolph is sure to get everyone riled up again. Can't let Serenity get too serene, now, can we?'' Derek grinned.

''At least wait until the judge and Sunny squeeze in a trip to England before things go straight to hell in a hand basket, okay?''

Derek looked confused. ''England?''

''It's a garden thing.'' Brice gave Derek an I-don't-get-it-either look, then said, ''Well, now, since you and Sally are aiming to get serious and cause a whole new set of problems, I suppose I should work on the present one and knock Bob Randolph's claim to the Half-Circle ten ways to Tuesday.''

Derek gazed at Brice. Determination set his jaw. ''I can help, Brice. I really can.''

Brice slapped Derek's thigh good-naturedly. ''Of course you can.'' Brice forced a smile. Sharing responsibility of running the ranch was going to take some getting used to. *If* there was to be a ranch to run. ''I'll drive into Amarillo tomorrow and get one of my law school buddies there to give me advice on how to fight off Bob Randolph.''

''I'll hold down the ranch till you can get back. Don't worry about a thing. Good luck.'' He gripped Brice's shoulder in a gesture of affection. ''Things will work out between you and Prudence. I know it. She loves you, brother. You have to learn to trust each other to do the right thing.''

TWO DAYS LATER, Brice headed back into Serenity, having driven four hours straight through from Amarillo and his friend's law offices. Brice knew he had got some great help there, along with a job offer. He laughed at that one—him in a law office fit like a shirt on a hog. He squeezed his truck into an Unloading Zone in front of the congested courthouse. If he got a ticket, he didn't care. Today, that was the least of his problems. Securing the Half-Circle had top priority.

If that was true, then why had he spent an incredible amount of time while in Amarillo thinking about Pru? Probably more than he'd spent thinking of a way to save his ranch. God, he missed her. He just didn't know what to do about it.

He checked his watch. It was fifteen minutes till high noon and the start of Bob Randolph's day in court. Brice fastened the top button of his shirt and straightened his string tie. He put on his Resistol and grabbed his briefcase from the passenger side. Then he headed up the stairs, meeting Derek at the doorway.

"Good to see you, big brother. Got your battle plan ready?" Derek stuffed his hands in the front pockets of his jeans and assumed a nonchalant expression as they walked into the crowded courthouse. They stood in the main hallway that connected to the courtroom.

There was a glint of uncertainty in Derek's eyes that Brice had never seen before. His little brother was more concerned about what was happening today than he was letting on. Who could blame him? The Half-Circle was his home, too.

Brice said, "The case is looking good for us. Don't worry about a thing, okay? I've got it on excellent authority that Bob Randolph and his kin don't have as strong a case as they think. When Wes wrote that letter, he was trying to impress Eulah because they were lovers, or close to it. It was a letter of passion more than a recounting of history or a detailed journal or diary."

Relief brightened Derek's eyes and pulled his lips into a grin. "Now, that's damn fine news."

"Everything okay with the cattle and oil rigs?"

"Everything's right as rain, just like it was last night when you called. I can handle things, Brice. Just trust me."

"I do. I really do." And he did, but... For some reason Brice couldn't get rid of the "but." He'd overseen every aspect of the Half-Circle for more than ten years, now. It was asking a lot to share the responsibility. Did Derek know enough to take charge of some things? He had a good education behind him. He'd worked on the oil rigs while in college and been Brice's right-hand man for years. For sure, he had more training than Brice had had when he'd taken over the whole enchilada. Maybe…maybe next year. Yeah, next year was soon enough.

Derek nudged Brice's shoulder and nodded at the doorway. "Here comes Judge Willis, that old dog." Derek chuckled and shook his head. "Like Uncle Judd says, just because there's frost on the roof doesn't mean the fire's out in the furnace."

"What the hell does that have to do with anything?"

"Word has it that Sunny was over at Finn's the other day and bought—get this—a pregnancy kit. She bought three, in fact."

Brice felt his jaw drop but was too startled to stop it from happening. "Sunny? She's…she's…you're kidding, right?"

"Nobody seems to know for sure one way or the other, if she is or if she isn't. But Janet over at the library said Sunny checked out four books on pregnancy, and Thelma at Thelma's Threads said she bought the pattern for a baby quilt. It's mighty interesting, and it sure has given the town something else besides the feud to talk about."

Derek glanced at his watch. "Hey, we better get inside. Willis doesn't take kindly to tardy lawyers, and lately he's been more feisty than ever. This pregnancy thing's gone right to his head, or some other part of his anatomy."

Brice followed Derek, snaking his way through the

mob of people, taking encouraging words from some and offering reassuring words of his own to others. He saw his mother and aunt across the hall, and gave them a thumbs-up sign as they entered the courtroom.

He caught a glimpse of Sunny Willis. The judge and Sunny were having a baby? Weren't they a little old for that? Was it even biologically possible? Today the judge looked cocky enough for it to be very possible, indeed.

Brice tried to picture Sunny pregnant, and didn't have much luck. Then he caught a glimpse of Pru at the drinking fountain and pictured her pregnant without even trying. He could imagine her all soft and round with his child growing inside her. Heat pooled in his gut, and his desire for Pru barreled through him like a bronc busting out of a rodeo gate.

He was in love with Pru. Even though he couldn't trust her because she was a Randolph, even though she would always choose her family over him, he loved her with all his heart.

But what in Sam Hill could he do about it?

PRUDENCE TOOK ANOTHER SIP of water, then watched Brice enter the courtroom. She still couldn't believe she was having his baby, though every time she tossed her cookies she was a little more convinced. It was just her luck to get morning sickness—that was, in fact, all-day sickness—right off the bat. The upheaval in her life wasn't helping, either.

She loved Brice, no doubt about that, and he'd

make a great dad. A baby—his baby—would be the epitome of family for him. Trouble was, there were two families involved. And they didn't get along.

Sunny waved from across the hallway, catching Prudence's attention, then came over. She cast a quick look around. "Gossipmongers are everywhere." She put herself between Prudence and the crowd, and whispered, "Did you give Brice the good news yet?"

"Now is not the time. He's got problems enough at the moment, and I've been no help at all in trying to figure out this letter business. Eulah's stonewalling me and won't give me a straight answer about anything. All I can figure is she and Wes were sweethearts that summer she spent with the Dillards while her parents were in Europe, between her junior and senior year of college. Then she graduated and married Thomas Randolph like her mama wanted her to and Wes married Gloria, a shirttail McCormack relative. Eulah's not going to say anything to help the McCormacks because she's been a Randolph for fifty years, but she can't bring herself to sanction the letter because she once loved Wes. That puts her in pretty much the same dilemma I'm in."

"It's sure not doing much to end this feud. I can tell you that much."

"How can Brice and I raise a baby surrounded by warring families? When I close my eyes, I keep seeing one of those political cartoons with a baby, arms outstretched, McCormacks pulling on one side and

Randolphs pulling on the other. I'm thinking about leaving Serenity, Sunny."

"What?"

"Shh. It would be for the best. After this is over, I'll just leave town. I'll tell Brice when the baby's born. He can visit whenever he wants."

Sunny snickered. "You really think Brice McCormack, high priest of all things McCormack, is going to be content with just visiting his firstborn?"

"Then what do you suggest?"

"I suggest you do nothing right now. Word has it he's been in Amarillo for the past two days, so he's got some plan cooking, I'm sure. If Brice keeps the ranch, you two will be able to work something out." Sunny patted Prudence's hand. "Stranger things have happened."

Prudence suddenly felt a smile creep across her lips. "Like *you* getting pregnant?"

"Having a little fun with the gossipmongers tickles me and the judge to no end. Now let's go find a seat near the back of the courtroom, out of the line of fire, and keep our fingers crossed for an end to this here feud. I had my passport photo taken yesterday, and I look right cute. The judge and I just have to get to England this year. The poppies will be blooming in six weeks, and I intend to be there to see it."

Sunny followed Prudence into the courtroom and found a seat near the door. The judge came into the room, snapping everyone's attention to the front. Feet shuffled as the bailiff commanded everyone to rise. There was a spring in the judge's step and a mischievous smile on his lips. Guess a man never got too old to be proud of his...sexuality. Prudence cast a quick look at Sunny, taking in her perfect appearance of hairdo, makeup and new suit. A woman never got too old to be proud of her sexuality, either.

Prudence and everyone else sat, then listened to Judge Willis's opening statement about how this better be worth the court's time or there would be hell to pay. Her father stood and waxed eloquent about the Randolphs being swindled, underpaid and lied to. Then he brought out the letter and waved it in the air. "And, Your Honor, I have here a letter written by Wes McCormack to Eulah Shelton...actually her name was Eulah Fairmont at the time, saying that Cilus McCormack did indeed know about oil being on the Half-Circle before he bought out Jacob Randolph's share of the ranch."

Out of the blue, Granddad Wes suddenly stood and said, "Your Honor, I've got something to say about all this here malarkey Bob Randolph is spouting."

The judge banged his gavel. "You'll be getting your turn, Wes. Sit down."

"Now, Judge, this here's mighty important to the case, or I wouldn't be here wasting your time and everyone else's." He nodded at Bob Randolph. "It's important to the part of the case he's talking about right now. Fact is, what I got to say will put a new edge on things and give everyone concerned something to gnaw over."

Judge Willis sat back in his black leather chair and

frowned. "Since this here's more of an informal hearing just to figure out if there's evidence enough to warrant a trial, you can go ahead, Wes. But I'm giving you fair warning. It had better be damn good, and you better be quick about it, or I'm shutting you down faster than you can spit."

Granddad Wes cleared his throat. "The way I'm understanding what Randolph here's saying is that his family wants part of the Half-Circle back because he thinks he's got it coming to him. Is that pretty much it in a nutshell?"

"What's the point, Wes?"

"Well, confound it, Jacob Randolph was paid good money for his half of the ranch. If the Randolphs are feeling like they're entitled to a portion of the Half-Circle, then that must mean the McCormacks are entitled to half of what the Randolphs bought with the money they got for their share of the ranch. I'm thinking maybe Randolph here can cough up half share in The First National Bank of Serenity, Randolph Feed and Grain, and maybe make McCormacks part owner of that big, fancy house the Randolphs have over on Elm Street."

Bob Randolph turned white, then red, intensifying to purple. Prudence sat on the edge of her chair. The courtroom was dead quiet, until Bob Randolph blurted, "What the hell are you talking about, Wes?"

"Same thing you're talking about, Bob. Seems to me you can't have the money for the Half-Circle and the Half-Circle, too. You get one or the other, not both."

Bob Randolph choked. ''That's the most pin-headed thing I ever heard of. The paltry money your great-granddaddy gave mine was just the beginning of the holdings the Randolphs have. My family has worked their behinds off to get what they have. You and your kin have no claim on that whatsoever.''

Wes put his hands to his hips. ''You can argue until doomsday about that, but the bottom line is that your family used the money to get a start. If you're claiming part of the Half-Circle the way it is today, then we can gosh darn claim part of Randolph Incorporated. Seems only fitting, if you ask me.'' He faced Willis. ''Fair's fair, Judge. What's the verdict?''

''Well, this does put a new wrinkle in things. I hadn't thought of the situation quite like that before. You got a point there, Wes. I'll have to think about it, check the legalities of—''

''Wes is right,'' someone yelled out.

From the other side of the courtroom came ''In a pig's eye. McCormacks aren't entitled. Randolphs worked to get where they are today.''

Uncle Judd stood up. ''And McCormacks didn't work to make the Half-Circle bigger and better?''

Judge Willis's gavel banged three times. Two Randolphs ignored the banging and stood, voicing their outrage over this sudden turn of events.

''Enough,'' bellowed the judge, as three more McCormacks stood in support of Wes and two stood to support Bob. Suddenly everybody was standing and shouting accusations, waving their arms and pointing to one side of the courtroom or the other.

The judge banged and yelled, and was completely ignored by everyone. Prudence watched Brice yelling at her dad and her dad yelling back. The uproar was migraine-quality and getting worse. She exchanged hopeless looks with Sunny and whispered, ''It's over. There's never going to be peace. No way can I stay here, Sunny. I'm leaving Serenity. There's no other option. This is no place to raise my baby. I've made up my mind.''

Prudence got up to leave, but Sunny took her hand and pulled her back down. Sunny nodded at the crowd. ''I think you should tell them all how you feel. They need to know, because way deep down inside I think a lot of people feel just like you do. Look around—not everybody's duking it out. A little grassroots support is what both families need to see how senseless this feud really is.''

''Like anyone's going to listen to me. They can't hear me above this din.''

''They'll listen—that I can guarantee you.'' Sunny gave a wicked smile. ''I was expecting something like this to happen, so I packed my persuader.'' She slid from her purse a can with a horn mounted on top. ''Meet the persuader.''

''What is it?''

''Foghorn. Press the little red button on top, and you'd think an ocean liner is coming right at you. I use it to persuade the neighbor's ill-mannered dog from our yard. He does his business in my petunias, of all things. Can you imagine? It'll get everyone's attention, sure enough.'' Sunny smiled sweetly, then raised her hand slightly into the air. With everyone else's hands flying in all directions, she fit right in. ''Better cover your ears, dear.''

Then she pressed the button, and it sounded as if the *QE II* was docking right smack in the middle of the courtroom.

Everyone froze in place, and Sunny quickly dropped the can back into her purse, fluffed her hair and assumed her sophisticated appearance as the judge's genteel, president-of-the-garden-society wife who just might be pregnant and would never in a million years cause a commotion.

Prudence peered at the McCormacks and Randolphs in their present frozen cameos. Pent-up anger that had been brewing for years overrode every other emotion she felt. Not only had she been defending her family and battling with McCormacks for as long as she could remember, but also choosing between them had cost her the man she loved. She was plumb fed up.

Holding on to Sunny's shoulder for support, she stepped up onto the bench where she'd been sitting and glared at the crowd. ''What is wrong with all of you? You're ruining Serenity. Don't you all understand that? Serenity's a great town, the best. It deserves better. Do you all like living like this? Well, I don't, not at all.'' She took a deep breath, feeling all the fight drain out of her. She was bone-weary. ''I can't do this anymore. I can't take sides between the McCormacks and the Randolphs. You can all slug it out forever for all I care. My baby and I are leaving this feud and Serenity, and we're not coming back.''

Chapter Twelve

For a moment Brice felt as if the whole courtroom tilted. Pru—his Pru—was leaving Serenity? And what was this about a baby? Pru was having his baby? He watched her elbow her way through the back of the crowded courtroom. Everyone was oddly silent, as if they couldn't quite believe what was going on. Prudence was pregnant with a Randolph-McCormack child. And she was leaving Serenity and taking the Randolph-McCormack child with her. Randolphs and McCormacks didn't leave Serenity. They stayed here, married and raised more Randolphs and McCormacks.

Brice watched Pru reach the door, turn the corner and disappear from sight. Holy hell! What was he doing just standing here like a fencepost? He started after her, stepping around the befuddled onlookers that clogged the aisle. Damn it all, why did Pru have to sit in the back while he was in the front, and why was no one getting out of his way?

Brice finally got to the hallway and ran toward the exit. Shoving the large, double wooden door open, he searched the porch, steps and sidewalk for Pru. He looked down the street in time to see her Lincoln barreling out of town.

Keys in hand, Brice ran to his truck...except that there wasn't any truck—just an empty space by the curb. How could this happen? How could someone steal his truck right in front of the courthouse of all places? Where was the sheriff? What was Serenity coming to? Brice swore, swore again and rolled his eyes in exasperation, focusing on the Loading Zone sign and the tow-away warning underneath.

"Dad-blasted!"

Turning around, Brice collided with Derek. Derek said, "Did you find Prudence, and what's this about a baby?

"I need to borrow your pickup."

"You never said a word about the baby, not even to me, your best man, your brother."

He grabbed Derek by the shoulders. "I didn't know about the baby. I was too busy...with the ranch." He closed his eyes for a second. "I should be shot at sunrise for not paying more attention to Pru." Then he looked back to Derek and said, "I need your truck."

"Where the hell's yours? I just got mine back from you."

Brice pointed at the empty spot. "It *was* there."

Derek tipped his hat back on his head and grinned. "Well, doggies. I guess you've been towed, big brother."

"Derek, if you're planning on seeing your next

birthday...*give me your damn keys.* I have to get to Pru and talk her out of leaving Serenity. She's making her getaway, as we speak."

"Then, you better think of some mighty good reason to make her stay, 'cause you sure haven't so far. I'd say some serious groveling is in order." He reached into his pocket. "My truck's on the other side of the courthouse, *not* parked in a tow-away zone, I might add." As Brice grabbed the key and ran off, he heard Derek say, "You'd think a lawyer would know better."

Brice didn't need the smart-ass comments right now. What he needed was speed. In minutes, he was in Derek's truck, heading out of town. He had no idea where Pru was going. She could be on her way back to the ranch to get her stuff, or she could be in such a state that she'd say to hell with stuff and just keep on driving till she got to...wherever.

That thought made his heart lodge in his throat, because if that was true, he'd never find her. Texas was a mighty big state. Good gravy, what if she didn't stay in Texas? But hell, everyone with half a brain stayed in Texas.

He and Pru had just found each other. They were getting to really know each other and figure each other out. And after knowing her all these years, he'd fallen in love with her. Of course, he hadn't told her that. Instead, he'd told her he didn't care where she lived and that he didn't trust her. All of which didn't sound too loving.

But he did love her, and he had to tell her that all

those other things he'd said didn't count because he was a fool to have ever let her go. How could he have been so stupid? He cared where Pru lived, and he wanted it to be with him. And he did trust her. He trusted her to do the right thing, the way she saw it at the time. No one could do better than that.

He'd never met anyone stronger than Pru. It was one of the things he loved about her most. That, and the way she made love with him with her cowgirl hat on. In spite of his present situation, a grin split his face, followed by a sharp pain in his gut at the realization that he might lose her before he could set things to right.

The back of the truck fishtailed, kicking up gravel, as he swung into the lane that led to the ranch. He rounded the first bend and spotted Pru's Lincoln parked in the drive. He thought he'd die from the sheer relief of finding her just where he wanted her most, at her house on his ranch. He skidded to a stop, killed the engine and took off for the house. He cleared all the front steps in one leap, and flung open the front door.

''Pru? Where the blazes are you?''

''Upstairs.'' Her quiet, controlled voice trailed to him as if she'd been calling him to dinner.

In a second he was standing in the doorway to the bedroom, *their* bedroom. The window was open, letting in a soft spring breeze. A suitcase was half packed and clothes were strewn across the bed. His heart felt as if it were caught in a vise and someone were tightening it bit by bit.

"You...can't do this."

She didn't look at him but kept folding clothes and putting them into the bag. "You said I should live wherever I wanted, and I don't want to stay here. My family, your family...it's not working, Brice. I'm tired of all the fighting, and I won't raise our baby where it will be torn in two." She shook her head, and her hair danced across her shoulders.

She'd taken down her braids, setting her curls free the way she always did when she was at the ranch. She was barefoot, too, and he looked at her pink toenails. He loved the whimsical side of Pru, the tattoo, the excitement in her eyes over simple things like her cowgirl hat. It was this unexpected side that made her happy and carefree, and made him feel that way, too. Life before Pru had been drudgery. With her it was pretty damn good. In fact, it was damn near perfect.

Her purple power suit was in a crumpled heap on the floor beside her high heels. She had on jeans and one of his green-and-white flannel shirts. Her cowgirl hat was next to her purse, car keys resting on the brim.

How could she leave this house, the ranch, him, and take their baby away from this place, when she so clearly belonged right here? "Where are the work-people?"

"Picking up the new oak bookshelves I had made for you. They'll be back tomorrow."

"Stay, Pru. I'm sorry for what I said. I care where you live, and I want it to be here with me."

She stopped packing for a moment, not looking at him but seeming to consider what he'd said. Then she continued folding clothes. "You're just saying that because of the baby."

"Is that what you really think?"

"Yes. You'd do anything for your family. And this baby is more your family than anything else in the world. You'd make our marriage work if you had to stand on your head every morning and whistle 'Dixie' with a mouthful of crackers. Anything to keep your baby here." She faced him. "Don't you understand that the baby is why I have to leave? I'm not doing this to hurt you, and I'm surely not being loyal to Randolphs over McCormacks. My father's going to have a fit over this...but that's too bad."

"What about living in Amarillo?"

"I was thinking New York City. It's the last place you'll find Randolphs or McCormacks. It's feud-free."

"You look pretty determined about this."

"I am." She picked up a pair of jeans, folded them.

He leaned against the door frame. "Almost as determined as you were that first night we spent here, and you were guarding that fire with the shovel. Remember?"

She glanced up at him unsmiling. "Of course I remember. But I'm not staying here, no matter how nostalgic you get."

He was quiet for a moment, hardly able to ask the

next question. "Do you want a...divorce?" He thought he'd choke on the words.

Pru stopped packing but kept staring at the clothes. Then she looked at him. Their eyes locked, and he knew all this was tearing her apart as much as it was him.

"No," she finally said, suddenly looking sadder than a withered daffodil. "I definitely don't want a divorce. Do you?"

"Hell, no."

A frantic honking of a car horn outside snagged their attention. "It's Dad. No doubt come to tell me I can't take his grandchild away from Serenity." She looked back to Brice. "This is one fight Dad's going to lose."

AS PRUDENCE RAN downstairs to confront her father—and a confrontation was exactly what this was going to be—she decided that if ever she was going to go insane, today was the day. She loved Brice, and there was no way she could stay in Serenity, and there was no way she could ask him to leave with her. He belonged here. He was the Half-Circle. It was his life as much as the blood in his veins and the heart beating inside his chest.

And the incessant pounding on the front door underlined just why she could not stay with him. Serenity had to be the most poorly named town in North America, she decided as she reached the bottom step. If a place was named Dry Gulch, you knew what to expect, the same with Locust Point and Chagrin Falls. Then there was Serenity. Ha!

"Prudence?" Her father's voice echoed through the house as he flung open the door. "Where are you?"

"I'm right here." She came to the doorway. "The question is, why are you here?"

"How in tarnation can you ask that, when you're threatening to leave Serenity with your baby—my grandbaby—and not come back? You've done lost your mind, girl, that must be it. You're not thinking straight. I hear being pregnant does that to a woman. I came to take you home where you belong, away from all this here confusion." His hair looked as if it had been combed with a vacuum cleaner, his tie and suit coat were gone. His shirt was half untucked. Randolphs in general were having a mighty rough day.

"You better come in and sit down," she said. Then she noticed Wes getting out of his truck, and considered the new wallboard and flooring. "Maybe I better come out."

She stood on the porch with her dad, watching as Wes stomped his way toward them. She sucked in a deep breath and stood her ground. "Dad, I'm not coming home with you. I'm leaving Serenity because the McCormacks and Randolphs can't get along. Or maybe it's that they just *won't* get along. It doesn't really matter anymore because I won't let the two families ruin my child the way you've ruined things for Brice and me."

Her dad looked at Wes. "What are you doing out here, you old geezer? This is none of your affair. Go get yourself lost."

"This here baby Prudence is carrying is half McCormack, so I'm staying. Besides, I wasn't about to let you come after Brice. We McCormacks stick together."

"I don't give a flying fig about Brice."

Prudence spread her arms in a helpless gesture. "See? See what I mean? Each of you is worse than the other."

Her dad turned back to her. "All I'm interested in is you and the baby, Prudence. I don't much care about anything else. The whole family just wants you to stay in Serenity. Can't have my only daughter and grandchild leaving me, now can I?"

Prudence caught her father's eye. He was telling the truth, she could see that, and it touched the very core of her heart. "You're not losing me, Dad. I'll always be your daughter, no matter where I live."

She heard the door open behind her, and she turned around and saw Brice, suitcases in hand, one hers...and one his?

Her dad asked, "Well, McCormack, are you fixing to just let her go? Aren't you going to do anything to keep your wife and child here? Least ways, if they're with you, they'll still be around these parts."

Brice put down the suitcases on the porch steps, settled his hat on his head and folded his arms lazily across his chest. "If Pru goes, I go."

Prudence looked at the cases and Brice. Then it

hit her like a charging Brahma bull. This was a great little bluff Brice had come up with. If Brice said he was leaving with her, both families would be losing out on their children and their grandchild. If there was ever a chance of ending the feud, it was now. She and Brice just had to figure out how to pull it off. Brice was positively brilliant!

Brice continued with ''Pru and I are leaving Serenity together, today. I have a job offer with a law firm in Amarillo if I want it. A friend of mine from law school. He said if I ever decided to give up ranching, he'd take me on. I've decided to give up ranching.''

Wes paled. ''This here's your home, boy. You've given it the best years of your life. All your kin's here. You can't just up and leave what you worked so hard to build. What's gotten into you?''

''Common sense. Pru and I are both tired of the feuding. It's destroying our life together, so we're leaving. It's as simple as that. We have our own family to think about now, and family is the most important thing of all.'' He looked at Wes. ''You're the one who taught me that, remember?''

Wes looked a little bleary-eyed, as if he couldn't believe what he was hearing. Brice was a wonderful actor; this was an Oscar-winning performance.

Wes and Bob exchanged a long look, then her dad said, ''Damnation! We're losing our children, McCormack.''

''Double damnation,'' echoed Wes. ''We're losing our grandchildren and their children.''

Brice reached for the suitcases. "And that's the way it's going to be because you two are more interested in this feud than anything else. McCormacks and Randolphs have been fighting for so long they don't know any different." Brice started down the steps and Prudence followed. "We won't raise our child like that."

Wes called after them, "Who in tarnation's going to teach my great-grandbaby to ride a horse, tell me that? He or she needs to know about the Half-Circle and all the kinfolk."

Her father chimed in, "My grandchild needs to know about Serenity and the bank and investing and...and how to play ball."

Wes faced Bob. "Didn't know you played ball, Randolph." He turned to Brice and Prudence. "Yeah, we need to teach the kid to play ball."

"And fish," added Bob with feeling.

"Yeah, fish," echoed Wes. "Who's going to teach the kid to catch catfish down at Willow Lake? Grandparents do those things. And all kids need to know how to swim, too."

"Swimming's mighty important. And kids need to go to Disney World. Ever been to see the mouse, Wes? We could take the tot to..."

Bob's words trailed off. For a moment Bob and Wes were quiet, the *we* word hanging in the air between them like a huge lasso, binding them closer than they'd ever been. Bob let out a weary sigh. "I can't lose my grandchild. I can't lose my daughter to a damn disagreement that happened seventy years ago. They're my whole life."

Wes looked at Brice, then back to Bob. He swallowed hard. "I'm not losing my grandson or great-grandchild. They're the only things I have that really matter anymore. I lost one person I loved over this blasted feud, and I don't intend to lose two more. No, sir. That's not going to happen." Slowly, he extended his hand, as Bob Randolph extended his. "Bury the hatchet?"

Bob nodded as he took Wes's hand. "Yeah, bury the hatchet, and for once, not in each other." The two men shared a quiet laugh, and Pru felt blissfully happy, almost giddy with relief.

What grown men and women had tried to do for seventy long years had been accomplished by one unborn child, the love of two families to keep their own safe, and a judge determined as all get-out to take his wife to see the spring poppies in London.

Brice set down the suitcases and slipped his arm around Prudence. "Think the two of you can persuade the rest of the families to go along with this monumental decision?"

Bob said, "It'll take a little adjustment, but if Wes and I want it to happen, by gum, it will happen. This afternoon we'll get both families back to Pine Tree Ridge to finish up some of the work that needs doing and have a dinner cookout. We'll get things out in the open and tell everyone how it's going to be from here on out, if that works for you, Wes."

Wes managed a twisted smile. ''Can't believe I'm having dinner with the Randolphs.''

Bob stuffed his hands in his pockets and rocked back on his heels. ''I'm feeling likewise, McCormack, but I'll manage.''

Wes scuffed his boot against the drive. ''Yeah, McCormacks and Randolphs will both manage.''

''We sure as heck will have our hands full convincing everyone the feud is over—except for the younger set, of course. They seem to be getting along.''

Wes snorted. ''That's the way the young folk always are. Heck, Eulah and I did the same darn thing way back when. That's what the letter was all about that I wrote to her. Great-Granddad Cilus McCormack really did know about the oil before he bought out Jacob Randolph. He told me all about it, and I told it to Eulah in hopes it might help end the feud with some sort of compromise, and she and I could get hitched. Then she wrote me back, saying that Great-Granddad Jacob Randolph knew about the oil too, *but* he didn't much care at the time because he needed ready cash to buy the Feed and Grain store in town. Jacob wasn't much of a rancher but he was one heck of a businessman. Cilus and Jacob became great competitors and did more to foster the feud than end it. I'm guessing Eulah never showed my letter to anyone, because it was only half of the truth. She's like that, you know. Fighting's okay as long as it's fair fighting. The reason we've tormented each other all these years is because it was the only way we could be together. Kind of strange, isn't it.'' He gripped Brice's shoulder. ''Glad you followed your heart, boy, and married Prudence—you didn't get cheated like Eulah and I did.''

Brice said, ''You know, Granddad, I'm thinking Eulah didn't turn over that letter a long time ago or get involved in Bob's court case now because she still has feelings for you that she's not ready to let go of.''

A twinkle suddenly lit Wes's eyes, and he seemed to stand a bit taller. ''You really think so?''

Prudence said, ''She never remarried after Thomas passed, did she? There's one way to find out what's on her mind—ask her.''

Bob grinned as he said, ''As I recall, Eulah usually takes a walk in the town square about this time of day.''

Wes shuffled his feet, then said, ''Is she still partial to yellow roses?''

Prudence smiled. ''Now that you mention it, I believe she is.''

Bob and Wes got into their vehicles and drove off. Pru and Brice watched as the Lincoln and the red pickup headed down the lane. Then they turned and faced each other. Brice's eyes were as brown as the earth he loved and as warm as the sun. His slow smile made her smile, too.

She said, ''What do you think about all this?''

''Incredible as it sounds, I think our baby just saved the day.''

Prudence patted her stomach. ''The real stroke of

genius was when you made everyone believe you were going to leave Serenity, too. Bringing down your suitcase along with mine was inspired. It made Wes and my dad really believe we were both leaving and that they would both lose their children. That equaled things out on both sides. What a great bluff.''

Brice tipped his hat back on his head, then tipped her hat back on her head. He rested his hands on her shoulders and he looked deep into her eyes. She felt a part of him, as if they were one in every way.

He said, ''For a lawyer, you haven't sized up the evidence too well. Pick up my bag.''

''Huh?''

He nodded at the suitcase. ''Pick it up.''

She did. ''It's...heavy.''

''I packed my things, too, Pru. This was no trick, no bluff. There really is a job offer for me, and I really intended to take it. You're my family now—and being true to the woman I love, pregnant or not, is what marriage is all about. I know that now, and I don't want you ever to leave me. I couldn't bear it. The Half-Circle is part of my heart, Pru.'' He kissed her. ''You are my soul.''

She was speechless for a moment, then said, ''You were really going to leave your ranch for me?''

''Like you were going to leave your family for our baby. If it's a choice between you or the Half-Circle, Pru, the ranch doesn't have a chance.''

She threw herself into his arms, nearly knocking

them both over. ‘‘I love you so much. I didn’t want to leave you, but I didn’t know how to stay.’’

He kissed her, a long slow kiss that made her forget everything but Brice. When he took his lips from hers, she said, ‘‘That was nice.’’

‘‘I’m glad you like it, because there’s lots more where that came from. This means we stay together, Pru. Our wedding vows count. Where you go, I go and vice versa.’’

‘‘How about we go to that tree over there.’’ She tugged him over to a grassy patch, and they sat down. A light breeze pushed puffy clouds across the blue Texas sky, and wild spring honeysuckle scented the air. She took off her hat, then his, placing them side by side.

‘‘Okay, what’s so special about under this tree?’’

She nudged him back onto the soft grass, then snuggled up next to him, her cheek next to his. Her hand rested on his chest, and she felt the steady beat of his warm, wonderful heart. ‘‘We haven’t christened this particular spot yet, and I think it’s time we christened every spot on the Half-Circle.’’

He laughed. ‘‘Pru, that takes in a whole ton of trees and hundreds of acres.’’

‘‘I know.’’ Now she laughed, then kissed him and looked into his loving eyes. ‘‘So we better get started, cowboy. Time’s a wasting.’’

‘‘At long, long last, Pru, a Randolph and a McCormack are in complete agreement.’’

HARLEQUIN WALK DOWN THE AISLE TO MAUI CONTEST 1197
OFFICIAL RULES
NO PURCHASE NECESSARY TO ENTER

1. To enter, follow directions published in the offer to which you are responding. Contest begins April 2, 2001, and ends on October 1, 2001. Method of entry may vary. Mailed entries must be postmarked by October 1, 2001, and received by October 8, 2001.
2. Contest entry may be, at times, presented via the Internet, but will be restricted solely to residents of certain georgraphic areas that are disclosed on the Web site. To enter via the Internet, if permissible, access the Harlequin Web site (www.eHarlequin.com) and follow the directions displayed online. Online entries must be received by 11:59 p.m. E.S.T. on October 1, 2001.

   In lieu of submitting an entry online, enter by mail by hand-printing (or typing) on an 8½" x 11" plain piece of paper, your name, address (including zip code), Contest number/name and in 250 words or fewer, why winning a Harlequin wedding dress would make your wedding day special. Mail via first-class mail to: Harlequin Walk Down the Aisle Contest 1197, (in the U.S.) P.O. Box 9076, 3010 Walden Avenue, Buffalo, NY 14269-9076, (in Canada) P.O. Box 637, Fort Erie, Ontario L2A 5X3, Canada.

   Limit one entry per person, household address and e-mail address. Online and/or mailed entries received from persons residing in geographic areas in which Internet entry is not permissible will be disqualified.
3. Contests will be judged by a panel of members of the Harlequin editorial, marketing and public relations staff based on the following criteria:
   - Originality and Creativity—50%
   - Emotionally Compelling—25%
   - Sincerity—25%

   In the event of a tie, duplicate prizes will be awarded. Decisions of the judges are final.
4. All entries become the property of Torstar Corp. and will not be returned. No responsibility is assumed for lost, late, illegible, incomplete, inaccurate, nondelivered or misdirected mail or misdirected e-mail, for technical, hardware or software failures of any kind, lost or unavailable network connections, or failed, incomplete, garbled or delayed computer transmission or any human error which may occur in the receipt or processing of the entries in this Contest.
5. Contest open only to residents of the U.S. (except Puerto Rico) and Canada, who are 18 years of age or older, and is void wherever prohibited by law; all applicable laws and regulations apply. Any litigation within the Provice of Quebec respecting the conduct or organization of a publicity contest may be submitted to the Régie des alcools, des courses et des jeux for a ruling. Any litigation respecting the awarding of a prize may be submitted to the Régie des alcools, des courses et des jeux only for the purpose of helping the parties reach a settlement. Employees and immediate family members of Torstar Corp. and D. L. Blair, Inc., their affiliates, subsidiaries and all other agencies, entities and persons connected with the use, marketing or conduct of this Contest are not eligible to enter. Taxes on prizes are the sole responsibility of winners. Acceptance of any prize offered constitutes permission to use winner's name, photograph or other likeness for the purposes of advertising, trade and promotion on behalf of Torstar Corp., its affiliates and subsidiaries without further compensation to the winner, unless prohibited by law.
6. Winners will be determined no later than November 15, 2001, and will be notified by mail. Winners will be required to sign and return an Affidavit of Eligibility form within 15 days after winner notification. Noncompliance within that time period may result in disqualification and an alternative winner may be selected. Winners of trip must execute a Release of Liability prior to ticketing and must possess required travel documents (e.g. passport, photo ID) where applicable. Trip must be completed by November 2002. No substitution of prize permitted by winner. Torstar Corp. and D. L. Blair, Inc., their parents, affiliates, and subsidiaries are not responsible for errors in printing or electronic presentation of Contest, entries and/or game pieces. In the event of printing or other errors which may result in unintended prize values or duplication of prizes, all affected game pieces or entries shall be null and void. If for any reason the Internet portion of the Contest is not capable of running as planned, including infection by computer virus, bugs, tampering, unauthorized intervention, fraud, technical failures, or any other causes beyond the control of Torstar Corp. which corrupt or affect the administration, secrecy, fairness, integrity or proper conduct of the Contest, Torstar Corp. reserves the right, at its sole discretion, to disqualify any individual who tampers with the entry process and to cancel, terminate, modify or suspend the Contest or the Internet portion thereof. In the event of a dispute regarding an online entry, the entry will be deemed submitted by the authorized holder of the e-mail account submitted at the time of entry. Authorized account holder is defined as the natural person who is assigned to an e-mail address by an Internet access provider, online service provider or other organization that is responsible for arranging e-mail address for the domain associated with the submitted e-mail address. **Purchase or acceptance of a product offer does not improve your chances of winning.**
7. Prizes: (1) Grand Prize—A Harlequin wedding dress (approximate retail value: $3,500) and a 5-night/6-day honeymoon trip to Maui, HI, including round-trip air transportation provided by Maui Visitors Bureau from Los Angeles International Airport (winner is responsible for transportation to and from Los Angeles International Airport) and a Harlequin Romance Package, including hotel accomodations (double occupancy) at the Hyatt Regency Maui Resort and Spa, dinner for (2) two at Swan Court, a sunset sail on Kiele V and a spa treatment for the winner (approximate retail value: $4,000); (5) Five runner-up prizes of a $1000 gift certificate to selected retail outlets to be determined by Sponsor (retail value $1000 ea.). Prizes consist of only those items listed as part of the prize. Limit one prize per person. All prizes are valued in U.S. currency.
8. For a list of winners (available after December 17, 2001) send a self-addressed, stamped envelope to: Harlequin Walk Down the Aisle Contest 1197 Winners, P.O. Box 4200 Blair, NE 68009-4200 or you may access the www.eHarlequin.com Web site through January 15, 2002.

Contest sponsored by Torstar Corp., P.O. Box 9042, Buffalo, NY 14269-9042, U.S.A.

PHWDACONT2